That Summer in Provincetown

ESSENTIAL PROSE SERIES 119

Canada Council **Conseil des Arts**
for the Arts **du Canada**

ONTARIO ARTS COUNCIL
CONSEIL DES ARTS DE L'ONTARIO

an Ontario government agency
un organisme du gouvernement de l'Ontario

Guernica Editions Inc. acknowledges the support of the Canada Council
for the Arts and the Ontario Arts Council. The Ontario Arts Council
is an agency of the Government of Ontario.

We acknowledge the financial support of the Government of Canada
through the Canada Book Fund (CBF) for our publishing activities.

That Summer in Provincetown

CAROLINE VU

GUERNICA

TORONTO • BUFFALO • BERKELEY • LANCASTER (U.K.)

2015

This book is a work of fiction. Any resemblance
to actual persons, living or dead, is entirely coincidental.

Michael Mirolla, editor
David Moratto, book designer
Guernica Editions Inc.
1569 Heritage Way, Oakville, (ON), Canada L6M 2Z7
2250 Military Road, Tonawanda, N.Y. 14150-6000 U.S.A.

Distributors:
University of Toronto Press Distribution,
5201 Dufferin Street, Toronto (ON), Canada M3H 5T8
Gazelle Book Services, White Cross Mills, High Town, Lancaster LA1 4XS U.K.

First edition.
Printed in Canada.

Legal Deposit — Third Quarter
Library of Congress Catalog Card Number: 2015936498

Library and Archives Canada Cataloguing in Publication
Vu, Caroline, 1959-, author
That summer in Provincetown / Caroline Vu. -- 1st edition.

(Essential prose series ; 119)
Issued in print and electronic formats.
ISBN 978-1-77183-035-5 (pbk.).--ISBN 978-1-77183-036-2 (epub).--
ISBN 978-1-77183-037-9 (mobi)

I. Title. II. Series: Essential prose series ; 119

PS8643.U2T43 2015   C813'.6   C2015-902301-7   C2015-902302-5

For Arianne and Clara

Contents

*If you can not get rid of the family skeleton,
you might as well make it dance.*

—George Bernard Shaw

CHAPTER 1

Uncle Hai's Magic Wand

Daniel died prematurely 28 years ago. You'd think with time he would be forgiven. But no, there's no such chance. Memory and pride go back a long way in his family. I know because his family is my family too. We shared more than a grandmother, aunts and uncles; we shared a century of untold stories. Daniel was my French cousin. Actually he was only half French but his ego wished us to believe otherwise. Muttering French to himself was his way of showing off his Frenchness. Unfortunately, his extensive knowledge of Vietnamese swear words always got in the way. "Fuck your mother" in a perfect Hanoi accent always betrayed him. He could not hide the other half of his roots even if he worked hard at it.

Daniel passed away 28 years ago at the age of 30. To this day no one in the family mentions his name. Or if they do, it is only in reference to me. "Remember when he taught Mai to scoop the fish out of the fish bowl to let it dry to death?" they'd remind each other. "What a naughty boy, that Daniel!" always followed "What a naive girl, that Mai!"

As kids we could not escape comparison. Living in the same house made this comparison even more inevitable.

While I stayed a good child, Daniel didn't. At his best, my witty cousin created art out of nothingness. He'd twist kitchen rags into dolls' clothes while music flew from his chopsticks. At his worst, he became a brat, always getting into trouble, forever seeking attention. I wanted to disappear into the background whenever an adult entered the room. Daniel would go out of his way to earn a kick in the butt.

Yes, Daniel received more butt-kicks than the rest of us kids. Butt-kicks, face-slaps, skull-knocks; he tasted them all. The punishment often came from his father's swift hands. Our mutual Uncle Hai, a young army sergeant with the ego of a general, participated as well in these acts. My own mother also showed traits of this inherited family disease. Although she loved Daniel and spoiled him rotten, my mother didn't mind knocking him out when the right situation presented itself. "Spanking, like eating and washing; another daily ritual!" my mother would repeat this as in a mantra.

Uncle Hai, on the other hand, never bothered with mantras. He never said much. One minute he would be jolly drinking beers, the next minute he would be removing his belt. It did not take much for him to turn dark. But the belt straps paled next to the rifles. Daniel bore the brunt of Uncle Hai's sadism, but I wasn't far behind. He never actually hit me with a rifle. But the psychological terror he unleashed proved worse than any beating. He loved playing a game of 'Kill the Communist'. In this game, I played the communist while he, a soldier, chased me around the house with his real rifle. Once, he even put a handgun to my right temple after handcuffing me. "And that's for collaborating with the Commies!" he said through clenched teeth, a cigarette hanging from his lips. I had no problem recognizing Uncle Hai's posture. The gun to the temple? I've seen that photo a dozen times. It was front-page material in all the Saigon newspapers for weeks. Uncle Hai had a thing for media images.

He behaved like a boy wanting to play John Wayne. Except that this was no John Wayne. This hero of my uncle was none other than Mr. Nguyen Ngoc Loan, Saigon's chief of police and the most notorious communist tracker of all time. And I had to be the communist in this game. Of course, the louder I screamed, the harder Uncle Hai laughed. For reasons unknown to me, my grandmother never intervened in these torture sessions. She only said: "Tuk! Tuk! Stop screaming Mai!" before returning to her betel chewing.

Fortunately, Uncle Hai also cultivated a civilized side. Being a doctor as well as a soldier, he sometimes healed people, not just threatened them. In a country of mostly emasculated-looking men, Uncle Hai's commanding stature and bulging pectorals drove women wild. So despite being a macho, all around town mothers stalked him for their daughters. Girls lined up in front of our house for a peep at him. I had giggling teachers giving me candies in school simply because of our family ties. "Tell your teacher I like her. Nice hairdo," my uncle reminded me often. The first time I blurted out the 'Nice Hairdo' line, my gym teacher took my hand and forced me down a dark, empty corridor. We walked for a long time in silence. Immediately, I regretted my stupid remark. I thought the teacher would report me to Mother Superior. But no, she spared me Mother Superior's rod. At the end of the long corridor, we came to a locked room. The teacher took out a key from her pocket, unlocked the door and invited me into her treasure cave. In the room, I saw new comic books on the table, sweet lotus cakes on the stove, candies in the open cupboard. The scene mesmerized me. "This is for you, but don't tell anyone," the teacher said as she handed me some chewing gum. After that episode, 'Nice Hairdo' became a sort of 'Open Sesame' for me. Every time I repeated it to one of my teachers, they would invariably smile. Saigon may have been big and overpopulated, but everywhere I went, I collected gifts from giggling ladies. Uncle Hai's magic travelled far.

⌒

How many hearts Uncle Hai broke, I don't know. How many hymens he tore apart, I couldn't guess. But there must have been plenty, given the perfumed envelopes in our mailbox each day. Uncle Hai never bothered with the letters, he only kept the photos. Snapshots of women adopting the Brigitte Bardot in *Paris Match* poses filled a box under his bed. Even in our society of restraint and self-denial, girls lined up to be conquered by Uncle Hai's magic wand. And the more he brandished his magical rod, the more those Nice Hairdos clung to him. He bedded indiscriminately: cute ones, plain ones, young ones, old ones. He didn't earn the nickname Horny Hai for nothing. Perhaps the war had something to do with it. Perhaps the war turned virgins into willing victims. "Procreate now before the war kills you!" It must have been a good pick-up line for the times.

⌒

Uncle Hai was my grandmother's baby and most spoilt child. She had him at the ripe old age of forty-two, which in her day was reason enough for shame. At a time when life expectation hovered around sixty-five, one became a grandmother at forty-two, not a mother. But my Western educated grandfather mocked this traditional school of thought. He had just returned from France an undecorated but proud soldier. Grandfather may have been a mere yellow-skinned footman doing the dirty work for the French during the Second World War. But pride still emanated from his every pore. Despite being an army doctor, my grandfather never had a chance to save lives. He did what was asked of him — prepping his diminutive compatriots for an encounter with the towering Germans. It was a thankless job. On his return to Vietnam, my grandfather marched triumphantly into the house, ordered *pho* soup from the cook and then love from my grandmother. It didn't matter that my grandfather's colonial troops failed miserably and France surrendered to Germany in 1940. Grandfather still felt elated setting foot on French soil to be part of history. So when Uncle Hai saw the light of day in 1941, he became not only a child of Desires Satisfied, he was also a child of Future Victory over Nazism. Even if my grandmother blushed over his birth, the family loved this last baby. And they spoiled him rotten.

Uncle Hai's childhood became the envy of his older siblings. The whole household put up with his whiny attitude. I guess being sick helped Uncle Hai's cause. At the age of three, Uncle Hai caught cholera like many other children of the time. The unyielding diarrhea robbed my uncle of his energy and roundness. His baby face turned angular as his skin dried up. Despite being a doctor, Uncle Hai's father could offer him no treatment other than bed rest and a liquid diet. In those days, antibiotics went to French patients first. Vietnamese, being second-class citizens in their own country, gave themselves opium instead. This by-product of poppy served many purposes: it controlled the people's pain, plugged up their intestines, lulled them to sleep and turned their despair into a fake euphoria. But opium remained off limits to three-year-olds.

Sick little Uncle Hai fortunately recovered from his cholera. This was a big deal at the time since many children in the neighbourhood did not recover. The day the diarrhea stopped, my grandmother gave a feast to Buddha while my grandfather celebrated with a whiff of opium. Contact with malady at an early age left its trace on Uncle Hai. Because he lost out on a few months of play, he soon became convinced the world owed him something in return. He developed an attitude of someone who could do no wrong. He took responsibility for none of his actions, caring for no one except his own cute self. A young Uncle Hai cried at the least frustration, knowing well his tears would break his mother's heart. When his new shoes hurt too much, he had to be brought to friends' houses on the maid's back. Pretending to be a warrior riding a horse, he'd stab the maid's ribs with his pointy shoes to prod her on. When nostalgia for his mother's breasts overtook him, my grandmother had to hide for a day. During this time away from curious eyes, she would tug like mad at her breasts. All this so she could squeeze a few drops of milk for her youngest son to suck when he should be out riding a two-wheeler. If he was a mama's boy before, Uncle Hai became the King of Mama's Boys after his illness.

With our family of mothers, surrogate mothers and nursemaids all living under one roof, the King of Mama's Boys wasted no time proclaiming himself the King of the House. Under his parents' colluding gazes, Uncle Hai reigned like an unenlightened despot for the longest time. But clinging to the same title at fifteen proved too much, even to my over indulgent grandmother. In the twelve years that had passed since Uncle Hai's cholera, many events occurred to change the course of history forever. While my grandfather had volunteered to fight under the French flag during World War II, other Vietnamese did the opposite. Using guerrilla tactics, these idealistic men fought for a Vietnamese flag, for a national identity, for independence from the French colonial power. My family, caught up in this tumultuous time, had its fortunes completely reversed. Like many other Vietnamese, my family experienced the war of independence first hand. This conflict between French troops and Vietnamese nationalists lasted many years. The two enemies exchanged bullets on a daily basis. Houses burned, babies wailed as cadavers piled up. In this setting, ordinary citizens morphed into agoraphobes. No one dared to venture far from home. They all feared being pierced by stray bullets. In town, people survived by lying low and munching on roasted rodents. Others evacuated to the countryside, filling their stomachs with leaves or rotting bulbs. Bloodshed, famine and despair characterized Vietnam of the early 50s.

The war of independence against the French finally ended in 1954 with a Vietnamese victory. After a hundred years of French colonial rule, Vietnam at long last felt the lightness of freedom. While ordinary citizens celebrated this new liberty, some feared for the future. They knew Vietnamese determination alone didn't win the war against colonialism. Chinese helmets and Soviet guns did. These soothsayers saw through Uncle Sam's distaste of communism. They predicted American apprehension would lead to catchphrases like 'The Domino Theory.' They knew American interventionist policy would not leave their country alone. The wise ones envisioned American B52s before they actually came and they understood that, from the ashes of this freshly won colonial war, another one would soon take shape. History books would call this new conflict a 'war by proxy' between the two superpowers of the time—the Americans and the Soviets. They would neatly file it under the heading 'Cold War'. Western media would refer to this bloody period as the Vietnam War. But in Vietnam, people called it the American War. For them, the war was not cold; it was very hot.

Like most wars, this war by proxy started as a war of words and persuasions. Anti-communist propaganda shaped people's thoughts years before American tanks descended on Vietnamese jungles. Socialist brainwashing proved no better. It instilled distrust while keeping people blind to the outside world. Communism and capitalism make bad bedfellows. So to accommodate both sides, the country split into two. The 1954 partition of the country uprooted countless families. Many Vietnamese from the north moved south to escape 'the Perils of Communism.' My family took part in that exodus — the first wave of Vietnamese refugees, spending the journey south in the belly of a cargo plane. Squatting on the floor, with her cloth sack squeezed against her, my grandmother tried contemplating her new life. But the sounds of the plane engine kept her preoccupied. She couldn't understand how a heavy machine carrying hundreds of people could float in the air. Surely, they'll all fall, she thought. And before Grandmother could spit out her nonsensical ruminations, nostalgia returned to haunt her.

Like many other Northerners moving south, my family left behind their friends, their ancestral homes and all their material possessions. My grandfather, who previously earned a living as a doctor, had a houseful of staff in the Northern capital of Hanoi. In the Southern city of Saigon, the family squeezed into a small, dingy rental apartment, courtesy of the International Red Cross. And this only for the first three months. After that, you were on your own. In the North, my grandfather projected the image of a respected member of society in spite of his opium addiction. In the South, he became a nameless, penniless refugee trying to claim a bit of Saigon for himself. With opium unavailable in Saigon, my grandfather turned to painkillers for his euphoria. Even as an unemployed doctor, he had enough medical connections to guarantee him a limitless supply of pharmaceutical highs.

Everywhere they went, my family and their Northern compatriots met resentment from Southerners — and rightfully so. Even without a penny, these new invaders from the North were not short on attitude. With geographic upheaval, economic uncertainty and social demotion all thrown in their faces in such a short period of time, my grandparents became less tolerant of Uncle Hai's King of Mama's Boy behaviour. At fifteen, they wished he would become a man.

My grandmother's daily tea offerings to Buddha soon paid off. A year after moving south, Uncle Hai grew from an effeminate looking teenager to a muscular, handsome young man. In growing up, Uncle Hai's attitude also changed. From an overprotected crybaby unable to assume responsibilities, he became macho. When his tears dried up, so did his vocabulary. His talk became so limited, they were practically predictable: *Hi Babe, nice hairdo. Love those tits. Give me one more beer. Shut your face, son of a bitch. Hey kids, wanna lick my boots? Yes, Mother. Don't worry, I'm fine Mother!*

Chapter 2

My Brother Tim the Tinker

My cousin Daniel died a young man in 1983. You'd think with time he would be forgiven. But no, he wasn't so lucky. Forgiveness only follows forgetfulness in our family. And instead of forgetting, we let ancestral memories haunt our nights. Instead of letting go of the past, we filled our heart with regrets. And no one regretted it more than my brother Tim.

Decades later, Tim still remembers his last talk with Daniel as a moment from yesterday. He remembers the isolation room on the sixth floor of the Montreal General Hospital. A summer sun oppressed the city with its heat but inside the air-conditioned isolation room, Tim shivered. He saw a quiet, emaciated body surrounded by fresh-cut flowers. The morgue-like scene shocked my brother. He thought he had come too late till he noticed Daniel's still-flapping nostrils.

"Happy late birthday. Sorry I couldn't come last week," Tim said softly, not quite wanting to pull Daniel out of his morphine stupor. *I'll just leave the gift here and tell Grandma that Daniel's OK*, Tim thought. My brother came only to do his familial duties. He would rather be with his girlfriend Susie, now that she had finally agreed to sleep with him.

Fourteen months he'd slaved after her for this moment; he couldn't afford to mess it up.

"I want to die," Daniel said, slowly opening his swollen eyelids. He looked puffy everywhere but underneath the edema you could see the irregularity of bones. Only a layer of serous liquid separated his inner and outer self.

You will die in time, thought Tim but did not elaborate. "It's no longer a matter of months, it's only a matter of weeks," the doctor had told Tim over the phone. But a busy school schedule prevented my brother from visiting until this fateful day. In fact, we all busied ourselves with daily routines too important to put aside. When we finally came with cakes, gifts and greeting cards in hand, we realized we had already missed Daniel's birthday.

"Your stupid sister Mai bought me a calendar for my birthday. What a gift!" Daniel said, waking up from his Demerol induced sleep. Yes, I did buy a calendar for Daniel's birthday. I did it for the pretty Monet pictures, something to decorate the bare hospital walls.

"She did it because it's cheap," my brother Tim answered with disgust. "Imagine, calendars in July, probably cost her ninety-nine cents!"

"No, she did it to remind me of my few remaining days," Daniel replied. "This family is rotten at the core. Lies can no longer cover the stink!"

Unlike Tim, my cousin Daniel had always been fond of melodramatic words. He had always been good at acting: shedding tears while playing Chopin on the piano, showering us with wet kisses at family reunions. We never knew what to believe, so we just went along with his show. It was easier to participate than to resist his phoney theatre of the absurd.

Suddenly recovering some vigour, Daniel licked his parched lips before letting out a barrage of secrets. On his deathbed, my cousin became a crusader fighting the myths

Grandmother had woven for us. Exposing our family's hidden stories gave comfort to Daniel's desperation. His heart functioned on revenge mode that afternoon. Fortunately, our family's tales of lament had never derailed Tim's tinkering mind. My brother remained indifferent to the world of gossip. As a kid, he'd rather take a clock apart than sit around listening to my grandmother's nostalgic words. When he took the TV apart and failed in putting it back together, we thought he'd kick his curious habit after the much-deserved thirty lashes. But he didn't. Machines fascinated Tim more than the rusty machinations of life.

My brother Tim is the youngest in our extended family of twelve joyless souls. Being the baby, you'd think he would be pampered like my Uncle Hai a generation ago. But no, Tim received the most knocks on the skull and the least attention. He was like a pebble that you kick out of your way. The only time you notice its shape is when it leaves a dirt mark on your new shoes. While Tim existed as a shadow in our family, he filled a real space in our Chinese maid's heart. She loved his handy hands fixing things in the kitchen. Her wizened maternal instinct slowly bloomed in Tim's presence. She'd protect him against Daniel's teasing. She'd shield him from the inexplicable family coldness. She made sure no one used him as a punching bag. In return, she asked for back massages and writing lessons. Like many other hired help, our Chinese maid could neither read nor write. To keep contact with her family in China, Nursemaid relied on Tim's penmanship for her letters home. Unfortunately, no common roots bind Chinese and Vietnamese writing — the former uses ideograms, the latter, Roman alphabet. But neither my eight-year-old brother nor my uneducated maid realized this. Undaunted by the lack of response, they carried on their task diligently. Month after month, they sent unintelligible letters to a perplexed Chinese family.

Our Chinese maid took pleasure in describing to her relatives our strange eating habits. She viewed Vietnamese food with disdain. Although she had lived half her life in Vietnam and spoke our language fluently, our maid still considered herself Chinese. Like most ethnic Chinese, she took pride in her Ming roots. Like most Vietnamese, we felt proud of our ancestors laying siege to those Ming soldiers. Whenever she could get away with it, our Chinese maid would cook us Chinese food. She'd leave the preparation of Vietnamese meals only for traditional occasions. Vietnamese or Chinese, it didn't matter. We craved everything she prepared. Unfortunately, most of the food went to adults first. By the time it trickled down to us kids, the food became a mishmash of unrecognizable shapes. It retained only a whiff of its original flavour, but it still tasted good, oh so good!

How much our maid got paid, I didn't know. Probably not much more than what a leper earned begging at the Central Market. Yet she didn't mind. The free room and board, sleeping on the kitchen floor and eating leftovers didn't compensate for her low salary. But the lively social interaction did. As a childless older woman, she enjoyed our house full of kids. She liked eavesdropping on secret conversations. She loved gossiping with Grandmother who claimed to know all the darkest corners of everyone's soul. With time, our Chinese maid became completely devoted to our extended family of brothers, sisters, uncles, aunts and cousins. We called her Nursemaid for it was easier to remember this than her complicated Chinese name. My brother Tim however called her 'ahma,' Chinese for 'mom.' This complicated business of addressing adults confused our naïve minds, so we preferred leaving it unquestioned.

Despite being thrashed as a child, Tim turned out fine. Despite the loveless upbringing, my brother did not end up joining some strange sect. Neither did he build bombs in bathrooms. His fascination for machines saved him from sorrows and self-pity.

From an abused Vietnamese kid, my brother Tim grew into a well-adjusted young Canadian man, top of his computer sciences class. Even his girlfriend Susie stirred our imagination. She sported the biggest pair of Oriental breasts we had ever seen this side of the St. Lawrence River. My randy Uncle Hai couldn't stop ogling her at family reunions. He tried waving his magic wand at her. But Susie saw through his games. She preferred my brother's innocent tinkering hands to my uncle's tiresome rod.

We all agreed North America did Tim a whole lot of good. There were machines here we'd never even heard of in Vietnam. Tim could spend days deconstructing then reconstructing meat grinders, pancake makers and potato slicers. He thought he had found happiness in Canada until that fateful day at the Montreal General Hospital.

&

Our family had left Vietnam one December day during the height of the Cold War. Getting out of shell-shocked Saigon in 1970 required creative planning. Even with the backing of our almighty American allies, the South Vietnamese regime daily lost ground to its Northern communist counterpart. To prevent people from fleeing an inevitable end, thus losing face to the world, the South Vietnamese government put a lid on emigration and foreign travel. Only those with connections managed to leave. The rest remained locked within a pressure cooker about to pop. Since my mother's social network stretched deep into the Ministry of Foreign Affairs, she got hold of passports stamped with exit visas. But where would we go? To America, of course.

My mother earned a living as a doctor in those days. She trained in plastic surgery, not to augment breast sizes, although there was a big demand for that even in time of war. She specialized instead in the repair of harelips and other congenital defects, preferring to leave the suturing of maimed limbs to her hardier male colleagues. Fresh out of medical school, my mother exuded idealism. She wanted to give a face to those perpetually hiding behind veils. She wished to see smiles instead of the ever-present hands shielding distorted lips. My mother also enjoyed practicing her craft on us. I became her favourite guinea pig. She tried enlarging my beady Oriental eyes, ruined the procedure and, as a result, gave me extra skin folds that added decades of winkles to my young eyelids. At ten, I didn't know any better. I thought it cool that my mother tried turning me into a white person.

When an offer to further train as a medical resident in North America materialized, my mother didn't hesitate to leave all her patients behind. She jumped at the opportunity to leave God-forsaken Vietnam. She relished bidding farewell to her long-suffering compatriots. Nobody blamed her.

After a week of packing suitcases and saying goodbyes, we traded the heat of an infernal city for the cold of a North American winter. The city we left behind smelled of diesel fuel evaporating from sordid alleyways where, at any moment, one could get killed or get lucky in games, love or drugs. It was a city that never slept despite the curfew and threat of falling rockets. From such a place of excesses, we parachuted overnight to a small New England town, paralysed by the season's first snowstorm the night we arrived. Derby, Connecticut smacked of cleanliness, quietness and safety. But since town folks discoursed only with those speaking their own accents, we soon found ourselves unwelcome. To the people of Derby, a gook remained a gook.

They saw no difference between a communist gook and a pro-American one. We all smelled of *Viet Cong-ness t*o them. Since the Vietnam War was still churning out American body bags, people naturally eyed us with suspicion on the streets. Indignant, the citizens of Derby asked themselves how the enemy found its way into the heart of America. We knew we had to leave fast.

Less than a year after arriving in Connecticut, we traded the New England cold for a more bitter cold as we headed north towards Montreal. In Montreal, my brother Tim blossomed into a computer whiz kid while Daniel's eccentric ways found a home on St. Laurent Boulevard. In strangely tolerant Montreal, my French cousin started to dress in skirts and became an instant star among his new friends. They applauded his daring fashion statement. In Vietnam, he would've been thrown in jail for this. In Connecticut, he would've been ridiculed, if not lynched. So Montreal became our home-away-from-home for the next four decades.

❧

"Our mutual asshole of an uncle, Uncle Hai, is actually your father ..."

Tim heard this from Daniel but the slurred speech convinced him it was the morphine speaking. *Daniel is hallucinating*, Tim told himself. *I'd better get away before he wakes up and complaints about being lonely again.* My cousin Daniel had always been the monkey of the family, always the one entertaining or shocking us with his tricks. As spectators, we had no idea how to entertain him in return. We couldn't lift his solitude no matter how we tried. We visited Daniel to show our solidarity. But we didn't make him laugh. Nor made him shed tears again. He had lost his sense of the melodramatic. Only raw anger emanated from his room on the sixth floor of the Montreal General Hospital. Anger alternating with morphine-induced snoring.

"Who told you that story about Uncle Hai?" Tim asked in a voice so low he had problems hearing it himself. Although my brother didn't quite catch the meaning of Daniel's revelation, his heart palpitated. He felt his irritable bowel syndrome resurfacing and knew he had to find a bathroom quick. Releasing a few wet farts became more urgent than listening to long-hidden family secrets.

My brother had developed irritable bowel syndrome the year after he graduated from high school. Before he actually found happiness in computer sciences, he drifted unhappily from one subject to another in college. Since we all expected him to build machines, he enrolled in engineering classes to please the family. When he failed his physics courses, Tim hid the failure from my mother, switching to computer sciences instead. Computer sciences, being an emerging discipline in those days, puzzled my mother. She couldn't understand all the fuss around these mini TVs. She wanted Tim to design airplanes, not write instructions for blank television screens. Living a lie gave my brother uncontrollable diarrhea. But in all fairness, I must say that my mother's opinions mattered less than she would've liked to believe. Tim's big-breasted girlfriend, Susie, probably contributed more to his sickness than my mother's disapproval. While Susie flirted with all the men around her, she flirted more with Tim. Susie recognized my brother's vulnerable soul months before he dared open his mouth to talk to her in class. And being the black widow spider, she felt no regrets exploiting him to his last hard-earned penny. But Tim couldn't let her go. He couldn't say no to a woman giving him some sort of affection. While far from genuine, Susie's attention fed Tim's starved soul. If he had depended on his family for spiritual nourishment, my brother would have dried up long ago.

⌒

By the time Tim returned to Daniel's hospital room, ass well wiped, my cousin was already snoring loudly. The Kaposi sarcoma had so deformed his face, he slept with one eye open. Tim looked away to avoid his cousin's glassy stare. My brother could not believe the changes in Daniel this past year. Handsome Daniel turning into a balding skeleton. Fashionable Daniel now clad in a lime-green hospital gown. Vivacious Daniel slurring his speech. Tim wanted to wake Daniel up from his slumber. *Tell me that story now!* my brother felt like screaming into Daniel's ears. Of course he didn't. He didn't have the heart to bring Daniel back to a God-awful reality.

Instead, Tim went home perplexed. *Horny Uncle Hai is my father?* he asked himself. *And who told Daniel such shitty lies?* he wondered. My brother Tim disliked idle talk. In Vietnam, he'd only exchange confidences with our Chinese maid. When we left for America, she presented him with a bagful of toys along with a gold chain while the rest of us kids only got a pat on the head. Yet he cried inconsolably for his *'ahma'* throughout the whole plane ride. Without his *'ahma'* in America, Tim started talking a bit more to me. We would joke about the principal's crossed eyes or the neighbour's fat dimply legs. But we never shared our deepest thoughts. In Derby, Connecticut, my brother picked up the American habit of listening to loud pounding music. Unfortunately, no one in our family shared Tim's interest in American rock music. His fascination for rock 'n' roll, like his obsession for machines, sealed him off from the rest of the family. And, in his isolated world, he found protection from our family's poisonous stories.

Determined to uncover the truth behind Daniel's words, my brother Tim went to our grandmother asking for an explanation.

"You heard that Hai is actually your father?" Grandmother said. "Well, well, well. It all happened when your mother took her younger brother Hai to Dalat in 1960." She was about to continue but then changed her mind. Without another word, she returned to her praying. In Canada, my grandmother replaced her betel-chewing habit with intense prayers. And, when she prayed, she stopped talking for weeks. Tim wanted to confront my mother, but she worked out of town in those days. This was perhaps all for the better because my mother tolerated no confrontations.

Chapter 3

My Mother Lan

My cousin Daniel passed away 28 years ago. The premature death of a talented young man brought incredible guilt to the family. And no one suffered this loss more than my mother. My mother did not wail like Uncle Hai did at the funeral parlour. Yet her silence spoke louder than any sobs. On the day Daniel passed away, my mother didn't lose just a nephew. She also lost a son.

When his own French mother left him to return to France, Daniel could barely talk. At three, he only knew the words *'non'* and *'maman'.* *"Maman! Maman!"* Daniel cried incessantly the evening his mother took off on an Air France flight. His midnight tears prevented the family from sleeping. But a guilty sorrow immobilized them. No one came to comfort little Daniel that night. My cousin refused to eat for four days after. My grandmother offered him her breasts but he only tugged at them angrily. He found no comfort in her dried-out sagging nipples.

Daniel's nocturnal cries for his French mother eventually ceased. In our large extended family living under one roof, finding a surrogate mother posed no problem. My grandmother would have loved to assume the leading role, but Daniel refused to play her game. Grandmother was too old, plain and backward for Daniel. As a replacement for his deserting French mother, Daniel preferred my own mother — a young, good-looking, modern woman. Naturally, my mother fell for Daniel's French charms. She let herself be manipulated by this wide-eyed kid with an upturned nose. But once in a while, just to remind Daniel of her superior position, she didn't mind giving him a thorough spanking.

With time, my mother became Daniel's unofficial adoptive mother. When he started calling her "mom" instead of "auntie," she didn't correct his mistake. Eventually she also referred to herself as his mother. This business of calling other women 'mom' was taken seriously in our family. 'Mom' meant love, but also power. The day my mother became 'mom' to Daniel, his own French mother got demoted to 'Catherine.' "Mom, Catherine sent me a postcard from France today," Daniel would tell my mother as my grandmother listened in on their conversation. To compensate for my grandmother's lack of status, Daniel would call her "Granny Darling, I Love You." This cumbersome title always brought a smile to Grandmother's wrinkled face. "Granny Darling, I Love You, can you buy me a sweet lotus cake today?" "Granny Darling, I Love You, can you do my homework for me?" At seven, my cousin Daniel already surpassed my poor grandmother at mind games.

My grandmother might have been an easy conquest for Daniel, but in my mother's memory, she played the tyrant's role. According to my mother's laments, Grandmother did everything wrong on purpose. She poisoned family dinners with maternal pettiness, berating when she should have been loving. She brainwashed her children with her ignorance, forcing superstition down their throats. She interfered in everyone's affairs, twisting their destinies like she twisted her braids. My mother and grandmother didn't sprout wings of love and respect. The repelling scent of resentment kept their souls on separate paths.

❦

My mother was the third child in a family of seven. She grew up in the northern part of Vietnam, the daughter of a well-off family. To say she suffered a traumatic childhood would be exaggerating things. But to dismiss her early years as being uneventful would also be wrong. Being the daughter of a young doctor, my mother knew no fixed address. As part of the first wave of Western trained physicians, my grandfather's good reputation spread fast. Grandfather followed his calling, setting up clinics wherever the need or money seemed greatest. The family travelled along roads barely worn. They went as far as the Chinese border and would have crossed it were it not for Grandfather's craving for Vietnamese *pho* soups. For her part, my grandmother at first missed the big city excitement of Hanoi. But with time, she adjusted to her new life amongst peasants. It gave her a sense of worth playing schoolmistress to a bunch of savages. She loved the attention and admiration of her new neighbours. But the memory of the capital turned her dreams to longings. My grandmother knew she would return to Hanoi one day to build her fantasy mansion. For this, she saved and skimmed every penny her husband earned. Her bank accounts were old socks with the embroidered words 'for Hanoi.' Her bank was the mattress on which she slept. With time, the mattress became lumpier as Grandmother stuffed it with more money-filled socks. Although my grandfather noticed the spreading lumps, he never bothered finding out its cause. Diagnosing lumps in mattresses seemed unworthy of Grandfather's talents.

Having no fixed address did not bother my mother. Growing up in a time of ambiguous loyalty did. As a modern man, my grandfather loathed all that smelled of traditions and thus Vietnamese. Whenever he could, he would send his children to French schools for a thorough brainwash. At those excellent French *lycées*, my mother learned that her ancestors hailed from Gaul. Weekly she sang *'La Marseillaise'* and spent her free time knitting socks for "our brave French soldiers in the trenches." Although she loved the cooking of her Vietnamese maid, my mother learned to dismiss the pungent *nuoc mam* or fish sauce at an early age. She replaced this popular local condiment with an imported staple: French Camembert cheese. Classier but no less stinky.

Unlike her classmates who mimed French ways without quite understanding them, my mother actually lived out her early adolescent years as a modern young 'French' lady. She rode bicycles when Vietnamese girls still hesitated to pose their virginal lips on penetrating saddles. She frolicked on the beach when all the women still obsessed about keeping their skin pale. In school, she talked to boys, laughing at their silliness while everyone else blushed at her daring ways. My mother's directness appealed to young men not used to such confrontations. They fell head over heels for her liberated manners, for her un-Confucius ways of thinking and her freshness of ideas. These idle boys of well-to-do families, still ignorant of the force of history that would soon hit them, followed my mother everywhere. They sent her 20-page love letters. They carved her name on all the school's trees. They even staged mock self-mutilation sessions to get her attention. My mother never fell for any of these tricks. She thought the boys stupid. None of them interested her but she liked the attention. In school, girls also showered my mother with praises. They all wanted to snatch her for their brothers, their male cousins, their single uncles. Fame travelled fast and, before my mother understood her fate, matchmakers stormed into her life.

One of my mother's most insistent pursuers was a 22-year-old young man by the name of Nam. At five feet two and with shoots of wiry hair sprouting from his skull, Nam was no beauty. He represented ugliness in my mother's eyes, but to my grandmother he symbolized good fortune. His family owned vast amounts of farmland around Hanoi. Nam also had the 'good luck' of growing up without a mother. Raised by two aunts standing in for a dead mother, Nam knew not the fate of a spoiled mama's boy. His father's fortune never hijacked his decency. His melancholic early start in life left him indifferent to money and titles. He only yearned for the love of a woman to fill the void left by his departed mother.

"So what if he looks like a monkey and scratches his legs incessantly in public?" Grandmother would respond to my mother's complaints. "The uglier, the better! No other girls looking at him. No fear he runs off with other women. You are so lucky!" my grandmother insisted but my mother, being a headstrong fifteen-year-old girl, was equally pig-headed. "No! No! No!" she answered every time my grandmother tried arranging a tea pouring ceremony for Nam. When my mother refused twice to serve tea to one of her most diligent suitors, my grandmother had to excuse herself repeatedly to Nam's father. She had lost face in front of one of the richest men in Hanoi and this made her blood boil.

For months, my grandfather didn't interfere in this matter of choosing a husband for his daughter. He took pride in his liberated, modern way of thinking. After all, fixed marriages were nothing more than a feudal exchange of goods and Grandfather considered himself beyond that. But my grandmother started nagging him about the war. The Second World War didn't spare our miserable country. Strategically located in China's rear end, our miserable country was seen as a convenient launching pad for expansionist Japan eager to slay the Dragon at its weakest point — its ass. History didn't rely on luck for its march — it functioned instead on backdoor deals. When France came under German occupation in 1940, a deal was made to allow Hitler's ally free access to Indochina. So with France's tacit agreement, thousands of Japanese troops descended on a Vietnam already worn out by years of foreign domination.

The Japanese occupation of South East Asia disturbed Grandmother's sleep. Not that she understood what went on. She didn't. She'd only heard rumours here and there. One day, Grandmother did catch a glimpse of two Japanese soldiers on the street. Their eyelids drooped so low she could hardly see the whites of their eyes. With heavy rifles fastened to their sides, they walked more like wooden soldiers than real ones. This sight confirmed Grandmother's worse fears: the Japanese were not human. At home, my grandmother painted such an exaggerated portrait that my grandfather had to pay attention. Grandmother also repeated a hundred times the rumours she heard at the market that day. "The Yellow Menace have no heart! They feel no pain! They slash their own bellies with knives! Yes! They called it hara-kiri! But I don't know what's so haha about it! The Yellow Menace bury Vietnamese alive! They stuff horses' innards with human bodies! They rape Vietnamese girls! Girls need husbands to protect them from the Yellow Menace!"

My grandfather didn't quite believe that bit about stuffing horse bellies with human meat. But the raping of young girls concerned him, especially with four young unmarried daughters at home. Middle age had caught up with Grandfather. He no longer had the energy to defend his daughters' virginity from ravenous soldiers. So, who would guard all these teenage hymens? When pressed into a corner, my grandfather had to admit the usefulness of the traditional marriage. In times of turmoil, love mattered little. Falling in love before the wedding became an outlandish idea. Like many men of his generation, Grandfather could not envision women taking care of themselves. Yes, young girls indeed need husbands to protect them! And so it was Japanese soldiers who sealed my mother's fate.

My grandparents arranged the marriages of their three oldest daughters in a matter of months. My mother rebelled but her rebellion went nowhere with my stone-faced grandmother in charge of the house. To quiet the arguments of her headstrong daughter, my grandmother only had to say: "I'll die if you don't marry this man!" This typical blackmail always worked in her household. Despite her initial protests, my mother ended up marrying her most ardent admirer, the ape-like man called Nam.

The wedding wasn't a small affair, as weddings in time of war should be. My grandmother managed to hire the best cooks to prepare the traditional roast piglet and fish bladder stew. A long table accommodating two dozen stretched from the living room to the yard. The ceremony lasted two days: the first day saw male guests, the second day female ones. On the 'male' day, a cousin of Nam's caught my mother's attention. His handsome angular face, punctuated by a beauty mark on the chin, brought a twitch to my mother's unsmiling mouth. Handsome Cousin also noticed my mother. One returned glance sufficed to convince Handsome Cousin. He saw through the wedding charade. He recognized my mother's unhappiness. Unable to control himself, he fell in love with my mother on her wedding day.

Although my mother managed to keep a straight face throughout the ceremony, she sprouted goose bumps beneath her golden silk tunic. She dreaded the moment when her future husband would touch her. She thought vaguely about Handsome Cousin, then dismissed him too. No, she didn't want to be anyone's wife. She just wanted her freedom back. Her wedding day became one of the saddest days of her life. Handsome Cousin also experienced a deep melancholy sitting across the table from my mother. He knew fate wouldn't be good to him. He knew he would spend his whole life waiting for this married woman. He knew she would be too decent to leave her husband for him. But it was already too late. Handsome Cousin had fallen for my mother. He couldn't forget her desolate eyes. So he sat down to write his first 20-page love letter that very night.

After the wedding, my mother bid goodbye to her family. At 15, she became a Mrs. Nguyen, wife to one of the richest heirs in town. But since money meant little to young ladies dreaming of muscles, my mother spent her wedding night cursing her own mother. My grandmother, for her part, congratulated herself for arranging so many weddings in such a short time. Except for her youngest daughter Shirley, who still played with dolls at the time, my grandmother managed to marry off all her other daughters. They became the responsibility of their husbands now. If they got raped by the Japanese, it was no longer her problem.

Rapes perpetrated by Japanese soldiers occurred no more frequently than rapes committed under the French flag. While my grandfather could turn a blind eye to French cruelty, he wasn't so forgiving of Japanese crimes. The extent of French cultural imperialism stretched far. It made men fall in love with the ideals of equality, fraternity and liberty, yet turn them blind to the injustice of colonialism. My grandfather couldn't see this contradiction. Like so many other colonized men, my grandfather brainwashed himself into loving uncritically a country that was not his. In doing so, he had neglected his duties to his own land.

In 1945, lackeys of the French were not lacking. You could spot them everywhere with the tri-coloured flag stamped on their fronts. They took pride reciting Verlaine or

Molière to each other. They learned to dance waltzes in tiny Chinese style living rooms to impress their friends. Yet, despite their Western hungry ways, many of these men couldn't give up one Oriental vice: the opium pipe. At first they smoked socially to relax. Eventually addiction showed its ugly face.

While some men lulled themselves to sleep, others plotted revolution. Unbeknownst to the French lackeys shamelessly betraying their country, another group of Vietnamese bred underground. These were young students, intellectuals, radicals and nationalists who objected to the French presence in Vietnam. In the 1920s, they started as a bunch of disparate dreamers secretly plotting midnight revolutions in distant villages. They worked in constant fear of their French oppressors, who as inventors of the guillotine, did not shy away from sharpening their tools. But history handed the rebels a trump card during the Second World War. During the years of Japanese occupation, when French attention in Indochina lapsed, the rebels boldly regrouped on the outskirts of Hanoi. After the Japanese surrender of August '45, French troops returned to a starkly different Vietnam, a Vietnam their advisers had reluctantly predicted but nobody took seriously. It was a Vietnam so hostile they had to wonder what had gone wrong? Which faux pas did they commit to breed such committed enemies? The enemies, invigorated by years of training, now lurked outside Hanoi's gate, ready to strike. The French felt no urge to embark on another war so soon after WWII. However, they had little choice but to follow the dictates of the time. The 'enemy' took on the name 'Viet-Minh' and their leader adopted as his *nom de guerre,* Ho Chi Minh. The rest, as my mother would say, is history.

Unsuspected by my grandfather, his firstborn son Tan flirted with this underground revolutionary group. While he lacked the discipline to become a true warrior, my Uncle Tan remained a fervent supporter of the nationalist cause. At home, no one noticed when Uncle Tan missed the occasional lunch or dinner. They assumed he spent time in opium dens. "That boy Tan is hopeless," my grandmother would say. "He's up to no good!" she would complain to my grandfather. But never did she expect his "no good" to be that bad.

Chapter 4

Uncle Tan the Sympathizer

My cousin Daniel died on July 18th, 1986. Forty days before leaving this earth, Daniel had a heavenly encounter with Uncle Tan. "Can't wait to meet you, Frenchy boy!" Uncle Tan said in the dream. "Been waiting so long for someone around my age to join me here. But this damn family is cursed with too many good genes!"

When my cousin Daniel reported this complaint from the grave to my grandmother, she didn't act surprised. And she didn't reassure Daniel that it was just a dream. Instead, she interrogated him for an hour. "Did Tan tell you when he died?" she repeatedly asked Daniel over the phone. "No, it was just a dream, for Christ's sake!" Daniel answered. But Grandmother wouldn't hear any of this. After all these years, my grandmother still didn't know how or when her firstborn son died. After all these years, she still hoped for a sign from him. She had no doubt he died. But how? And when? The 'how' seemed important the first few years of his disappearance. Later on, only the 'when' kept Grandmother awake at night.

Each year, my grandmother would celebrate the anniversary of Uncle Tan's death with a family get-together. She would cook Uncle Tan's favourite dishes, even setting a place for him at the dinner table. "His spirits will join us," my grandmother would tell us every year. At this special occasion, the family would eat, drink and discuss the high cost of food and gas. Remembrance lasted five minutes. Daily concerns lasted two hours. Our family had more immediate worries than to think about a distant disappearance. But Grandmother persisted in her belief that ghosts can eat. The date my grandmother selected to celebrate her son's rise to heaven remained an arbitrary one. She chose the day she last saw him in the flesh. But he could've died the following day. Or the day after. With time, my grandmother became obsessed with dates. She wished to know the true date of her son's death. She wanted so much to give him a proper remembrance feast each year. Yet how could a remembrance feast be proper if the death date stayed a mystery? In this matter, nobody could help Grandmother.

When my grandmother last saw Uncle Tan in 1948, he was a careless young man. By then, my grandfather had returned triumphant from his war effort in France, the Japanese had left Vietnam, the war of independence against the French raged in full swing and my mother and her sisters all lived unhappily with their in-laws. The French versus Viet Minh street fighting left Hanoi almost empty. Many civilians fled to the countryside to avoid being victims of stray bullets. Heeding their husbands' advice, my mother and her sisters walked for three days to find shelter in a rural plantation. My grandmother didn't want to leave Hanoi at first. She felt too attached to her home and worldly possessions — this despite being a devout follower of Buddha. She used my grandfather's illness as an excuse to stay behind. It looked good, a wife staying back to care for her sick husband in times of war. When the fighting intensified, my grandmother's common sense got the better of her. She too decided to bid her Hanoi mansion goodbye. During those fateful months of the war, my grandfather became afflicted with a combination of hepatitis, untreated hipbone infection and opium withdrawal symptoms. He was in a sorry state for a doctor and had no desire to leave his bed. Grandfather's wandering lucidity convinced my grandmother that safety lay under the blanket, not on the road. Before evacuating to safer grounds, Grandmother asked Uncle Tan to stay with his father. According to her Confucius logic, the oldest son belongs with the father, no matter what. Uncle Tan didn't protest this decision. His non-reaction was more a sign of commitment to the Cause than a sign of filial duty. Fleeing to the countryside meant cowardice. Staying showed solidarity. But my grandmother never figured any of this out.

Why did Grandmother leave a son behind when the French viewed all young Vietnamese men as suspects? Why didn't she arrange for a maid to care for my grandfather instead? My grandmother could never explain this to the rest of the family when they finally reunited many months later. When the battle for Hanoi cooled, my grandmother and her children returned to an eerily quiet house marked by a lone bullet hole in the living room wall. Aside from the bullet hole, the house looked unchanged. No blood stains, no crashed windows, no burnt-out curtains, not even a dent on the armchair to indicate a forceful fight. The smell of death permeated neighbouring houses but spared my grandmother's mansion. But where did my grandfather and Uncle Tan go?

When a tour of the city morgue proved unfruitful, my grandmother let out a sigh of relief. Next came visits to crowded hospital wards where moaning men and the visions of ghosts that died the day before kept my grandmother from concentrating on her mission. Distracted, she failed to recognize amongst the wounded three of her neighbours down the street. Bed after bed, my grandmother looked blankly at red-shot eyes that refused to return her stare. She walked like a madwoman from corridor to corridor calling out the names of her husband and son. While Grandmother recognized no one, fate had it that one of the French Red Cross volunteers recognized her as the mother of one of her students.

"I'm Mlle Caillot, Thu's old teacher," the Red Cross volunteer explained. "Do you remember me? Your daughter Thu was my best student. I hope she is fine. A French soldier brought your husband, Dr. Vu, here a few months ago. I recognized his bulging eyes the minute they wheeled him in. A bullet took his memory away." Seeing tears in my grandmother eyes, Mlle Caillot quickly added, "No, he wasn't wounded in the head! The bullet only scared him. He spoke perfect French so the soldier assumed he was on our side. They took him to the hospital because of his confused state. He's been discharged to one of your relatives. No, I don't know which one and no, I didn't see his son ... Please send my greetings to your daughter Thu."

"One of your relatives ..." Yes, but which one? Both my grandparents came from large families. And a cousin of a cousin of a cousin also counted as a relative. Curfews and the lack of phones made communication during times of war a Herculean task. But my grandmother never gave up hope. After four weeks of scouring a labyrinthine city, Grandmother finally tracked down her husband. Grandfather was on the verge of being kicked out from the home of one of his in-laws. Under their harsh care, my grandfather had gone from an incoherent lunatic to a withdrawn mute.

At home, my grandfather slowly recovered his facility for speech. At first, he only gave simple answers to questions that bombarded him from all sides. *Do you know where Tan is?* No. *Is he dead?* No. *Are you sure?* No. *Do you remember the bullet?* No. *Do you want pho soup?* Yes. Eventually Grandfather's full speech and, with it, his usual complaints and grumbling returned. But the memory of those days, when, deserted by his family, Grandfather alone witnessed the burning of Hanoi at the hands of those who loved it most, never returned. No matter how hard he tried, my grandfather could not remember what happened to his firstborn son Tan. The bullet hole in the living room also perplexed him. Too high up the wall to kill anybody. No, this bullet, fired so high up, was only meant as a warning. It wasn't supposed to penetrate anyone's viscera. If my Uncle Tan didn't die, why did he disappear?

Conspiracy theories fuelled people's imagination in those days. For every disappearance, a hypothesis popped up to give reasons to the family left behind. Those who opposed colonialism blamed French soldiers for their missing brothers. Those who distrusted the nationalists' overzealous fervour blamed the Viet Minh for their sons' demise. Rumours of French soldiers rounding up young Vietnamese men for mass execution abounded. So were tales of Vietnamese revolutionaries ridding themselves of the traitors in their midst. And in the middle of such drama lurked cowards who used this historical backdrop to disappear for their own selfish reasons. They were husbands lacking the nerve to come clean about their mistress in tow. They were weaklings not daring to speak out against the choice of brides their parents made. They were dreamers who could only travel in their opium dens. Now, with the old restrictive world disintegrating around them, these men had no reason not to flee. And they did flee.

My mother would like to believe her brother Tan belonged to that last group. She would like to believe he fled Hanoi, resettled somewhere overseas, and still dreamed but not under the influence of opium. My mother would rather he took a cowardly flight than die a martyr's death. 'Martyrs' deaths' and 'heroic resistance' became such popular words, my mother felt sick hearing them. She didn't want her brother's name associated with those hollow sounds.

My Uncle Tan was my mother's favourite brother. They both walked with the same elf-like gait. They both sported silky black hair flowing down their head like thick India ink. They both loved pulling tricks on their more serious sister Thu. While the family doted on the young Uncle Hai, my mother saw through his bratty cuteness. When the family berated Uncle Tan for his laziness, Mother defended him like only a younger sister could — with touching devotion and naiveté. She didn't worship her older brother; he had too many obvious faults for that. But she loved him wholeheartedly.

❧

Uncle Tan was my grandmother's firstborn. Proud to give birth to a boy when all her sisters had girls, my grandmother never took her eyes off the baby. She brought her son everywhere she went, even to the matrimonial bed where he would curl up happily while my grandfather fumed. Like many young mothers, Grandmother fell in love with this first son, so sweet and easy to care for. Much to my grandfather's chagrin, Grandmother spent more time coo-cooing her infant son than sweet-talking her husband. This supposed gift from God became a pest in Grandfather's eyes.

When Uncle Tan turned five, my grandmother took him to a fortune teller. Curiosity about the fate of her son led her to a dark, smelly room, a place she would regret forever after. When the fortune teller predicted Uncle Tan's early death, Grandmother didn't react with drama. She didn't indulge Uncle Tan with more love. She didn't protect him more. She became distant to him instead. Two years after the visit to the fortune teller, my grandmother put a lid on her maternal instinct. She locked her tenderness away somewhere and, with time, no one could find the key to that forbidden place. She thought, if she stopped loving her son, the hurt would be tolerable when he would be taken from her.

No one in the family knew of the fortune teller's prediction. They only witnessed Grandmother's harsh ways with her oldest son. Although they sympathized with him, they knew they couldn't change her behaviour. Whatever he did, Uncle Tan's actions would be met with parental criticism. To escape his parents' disapproval, Uncle Tan indulged in daydreams. He'd read useless poetry. He'd loiter unwanted around friends' houses. He'd skip school to try out opium dens. In short, he became the black sheep of the family.

Grandmother stopped playing 'cold and distant' with her firstborn the year he turned sixteen. By then, her aloofness toward Uncle Tan had become so real she no longer had to pretend. At home, even the servants treated Uncle Tan with disrespect. "Ah, the starving poet is home!" they would snicker every time he walked into the house. Instead of scolding the maids for their insolence, my grandmother encouraged them with her own rolled-up eyes. Only my mother understood Uncle Tan's need to escape. She didn't blame him for his lack of discipline. Instead, she found unforgivable her mother's negligence.

⁊

When my mother returned to Hanoi to find Uncle Tan gone, she could not contain her grief. She prayed for him every night. She held out hope of finding him again, but that hope grew dimmer with each day without news. Although they never found his body, the family eventually accepted the neighbours' theory of a French mass execution of young men. Nobody recognized Uncle Tan, but neighbours reported seeing young Vietnamese men being led away by French soldiers. Nobody heard rifle shots, but neighbourhood kids saw blindfolded people lined up against a wall. "Those sons of a bitch!" my grandfather screamed at this bit of news. Since regaining his speech, my grandfather couldn't stop cursing the French colonialists. Like his memory, my grandfather's infatuation for the French never returned after 1948.

My mother also cursed the French. But she cursed her own mother more. "Why didn't you take Older Brother Tan with you to hide in the countryside? Why didn't you arrange for a maid to care for Father instead of Tan?" My mother could pester all she wanted; Grandmother had no answer to give. The fortune teller's prediction finally came true and my grandmother was glad she'd cut ties with her son so long ago. She didn't feel much sorrow learning of his death through neighbours' rumours. Her only obligation now was to give him a proper remembrance meal every year.

When Grandmother forced a marriage of convenience on my mother, she protested but not too vehemently. Her favourite brother's death was another matter. She blamed Grandmother for Uncle Tan's fate. And the more Grandmother shrugged her shoulders, the more my mother resented her lack of reaction. From that day on, my mother decided to dump her mother's values into the garbage where they belonged. She would rebel; she would bring shame to her mother's good name. She yearned to break parental rules.

Chapter 5

My Father the Buffalo Boy

My cousin Daniel passed away 28 years ago in a Montreal hospital. To this day, there are acquaintances of the family still unaware of his death. "Oh, he left for Europe," his father would tell people asking for his news. "He went to search for his mother Catherine in France," my grandmother would quickly add. "You know, that crazy French woman who left him at the age of three!" Twenty-eight years after the fact, there are members in the family still refusing to mention Daniel's disease. "He has hemorrhoids ..." was the closest that Grandmother could come to naming Daniel's sickness.

Daniel's malady tarnished my grandmother's sense of symmetry. Her smoke-and-mirrors game could not mask the sight of disintegrating flesh. Her concoctions of lies fooled no one but herself. Although she didn't quite understand his lifestyle, she knew it to be wrong. When prayers to Buddha didn't change Daniel's ways, Grandmother tried ignoring the telltale signs. She reassured herself that everything looked as it should. Daniel's female friends all had big hands, deep voices and prominent Adam's apples, but Grandmother didn't mind. She thought his bunch of girlfriends charming.

She wished he had settled down with Marie, the blonde one with the big hairy arms. Marie's outrageous talk always tickled my grandmother's fancy.

When Horny Uncle Hai finally diagnosed Daniel's weight loss with a fateful blood test, Grandmother could no longer escape the truth. The newspapers had reported on this new sickness everyday and, being the wife of a doctor, my grandmother had read those articles with curiosity. It was information she wished she hadn't known. Imagine, her favourite grandson carrying the most shameful disease of the 20th century! This shame immobilized my grandmother. She hid from prying neighbours wishing to expose her dirty laundry.

Scandals plagued my grandmother's life. Although the first scandal crossed her path in 1960, Grandmother remembered it as an event from last month. That memory still gave her cold sweats. The force of history didn't spare my family; they struggled against the odds and survived one of the longest wars of the 20th century. But for Grandmother, the most important event after her son's disappearance was the Scandal.

After the French defeat at Dien Bien Phu, Vietnam experienced a period of both elation and confusion. A young Ho Chi Minh, disappointed with the Americans' stonewalling, deepened his ties with communist Russia and China. Thus, what initially started as a nationalist uprising against the French soon snowballed into a socialist revolution. Under the world's watchful eyes, Vietnam split into two in 1954. The Geneva Accord of that year allowed North Vietnam its socialist agenda while guaranteeing the South its market-driven path. While a million paranoid Northerners fled south to fend for themselves in a dog-eat-dog capitalist world, 50,000 idealistic Southerners relocated north to help build a classless utopia. My family belonged to the former group — confused Northerners fearing communist redistribution of land. They couldn't imagine sharing their house with five other families. So they gave up everything in order to find a bit of free-market paradise in the south. But most of them found only cramped quarters, inflation, unemployment, empty pockets and local contempt. The Southerners refused to roll out the red carpet for their Northern compatriots.

Not all Northerners shared this lousy experience. Some had the foresight to move south before the going got rough. These clever people bought southern land for a tenth of what the price would be after partition. They also had enough common sense to befriend the Southerners before they turned on you. My father belonged to that carpetbagger gang.

My father was born into a big Northern family more concerned with making money than making sense of the world. Since education meant little in his family, my father left school at age 10 to mind his water buffaloes. His parents owned a few dozens of these creatures as well as large amounts of land. They led a comfortable life exploiting their own children to save money on hired hands. Being the youngest lad in the family, my father got the easiest job, that of a buffalo boy. This chore gave him unlimited daydream time in the fields. So, while the water buffaloes digested their grass, my father plotted his first how-to-get-rich scheme.

My father exuded innocence, calmness and generosity. These were not great qualities for a businessman but Luck walked with him. All his projects turned to gold. He started by selling silk blouses to French ladies on the streets. "*Soie! Soie! Madame!* " My father would spend his days screaming these words on the streets of Saigon. Because he only knew these two French words, bargaining seemed out of the question. His prices were already printed on a piece of paper. When French ladies tried the universal sign language of 'give me two for the price of one,' my father only shrugged in confusion. Exasperated, the French ladies gave up their attempts at bargaining. They paid my father's fixed price and earned a smile in return. From a street vendor, my father became a storeowner. Later, he built hotels catering to American soldiers on R&R. In all his years of doing business, my father never lost a deal. Men trusted his quiet manner. Women fell for his looks and bank account. That he married one of the ugliest women in town only made bolder the ladies' flirtatious advances.

My mother never made inappropriate advances towards my father. In 1955, when she met him for the first time, she addressed him by the respectful but misleading title "Uncle Hoc." But my father was not my mother's uncle; he was her third cousin. When my family ran into tough financial times in 1954, Grandmother pushed my mother into her rich cousin's lap. "That illiterate buffalo boy made his fortune dealing with White Demons. Go ask him for help. He's my cousin. He won't refuse us," Grandmother ordered.

My father never turned down those in need. Generosity came easily to him. Generosity multiplied exponentially in front of pretty women. My parents met often to talk business. My father not only lent my mother huge sums of money interest free, he also gave her sound business advice. When *Aux Délices*, a French restaurant went up for sale, my father encouraged Mother to acquire it. Like many of their compatriots, the old French owners feared political instability in post-colonial Vietnam. They were desperate to sell the business. Taking my father's advice, Mother bought the restaurant and revamped it. She kept the French menu but made the place Vietnamese friendly. She fired the haughty waiters who acted as if they once hobnobbed with Jean-Paul Sartre on Montparnasse. She replaced these severe-looking Frenchmen with waitresses wearing sensual Vietnamese *ao dais*. To the Edith Piaf soundtrack, she added the occasional Pham

Duy songs. Pham Duy's nostalgic love ballads always worked. Patrons inevitably lingered on. They ordered more beer, hoping to catch another impossibly sad song. My mother's restaurant soon became a hit with Saigon's new jet set.

At first, my father wanted to know all the financial details of my mother's restaurant. When the restaurant became successful, my father would inquire about the social aspects of this hot new eatery. Who's having lunch with whom? The Minister of Foreign Affairs flirted with the waitress again? Did the Millionaire come today? My father loved gossip. My parents would meet late at night to talk shop. In the restaurant business, it didn't seem unusual making rendezvous after midnight. Before that ghastly hour, my mother would be too busy running the place to give attention to her benefactor.

Despite the odd hours, Grandmother saw my parents' meetings as nothing more than standard business encounters. After all, they were both married to other people and the same blood ran through their veins. Certainly, this same-blood business should suffice to temper all ungodly lust. My grandmother had no reason not to trust her daughter with her cousin. But my mother had other intentions.

When she first set eyes on my father, my mother immediately noticed his bear-like physique. Unlike the short, skinny husband she had at home, this big cuddly man left her twitching all over. Despite his buffalo boy background, my father had the same facial features as His Royal Highness Bao Dai, the last emperor of Vietnam. To most Vietnamese men, Emperor Bao Dai symbolized impotence. He was nothing more than a powerless puppet of the French regime. But to the majority of Vietnamese women, 'Bao Dai' rhymed with virility, charm and seduction. When it came to fantasies about emperors, my mother proved no different than the average Vietnamese woman. The Bao Dai features glowed in my father's face. The brown meaty lips, the prominent cheeks, the fine straight nose, the deep-set eyes, my father had it all. My mother blushed when she first saw her third cousin, the buffalo boy looking like an emperor. During that meeting, she giggled like a schoolgirl, losing all her composure. My mother's decade-old fantasies for Handsome Cousin evaporated into thin air after her first encounter with my father. The Bao Dai lookalike exuded not only good looks, he also handled money like paper.

When the Bao Dai novelty wore off a few months later, my mother began comparing my father to Beethoven. "It's the passion, stupid!" my mother would exclaim, trying to show her girlfriends the obvious link between Beethoven and my father. When the friends asked "Who's Beethoven?" my mother gave them a wicked smile. She loved tricking them into asking stupid questions. Their ignorance made her feel good about her private French school education. My father, the object of Mother's desire, also wondered "Who is this Beatovan?" "Never mind!" my mother would answer. The culturally deprived Buffalo Boy put her to shame at times. But his good looks and fortune made up for his lack of refinement.

For his part, my father was not immune to my mother's youthful charms. It was not the lack of sex that pushed him to hit on my mother. Being a man of means, my father Hoc had more mistresses than his wife had teeth in her mouth. Dividing his semen among the bickering mistresses while keeping a straight face at home became a hassle. He didn't want more trouble. But my mother, the forbidden fruit, deserved special attention. The daughter of your cousin, and a married woman on top of it!

It is not easy to hide lust. Despite their attempt at discretion, my parents' adultery became known. This earned my mother a much hoped-for divorce from her husband Nam.

My father was less fortunate. His wife clung to him like a leech after his scandalous affair became public knowledge. The wife also became my family's tormentor. "Your slut of a daughter is a bitch!" she would scream to my grandmother whenever their paths crossed on the street. She would stalk my mother for hours then suddenly reveal herself to make a public scene. "You miserable whore, you deserve to die!" she would shout before striking my mother with a wooden stick. She threatened to throw acid on my mother's face but never managed to acquire the right type of disfiguring formula. With the wife's penchant for public scenes, my mother's incestuous extra-marital affair became the talk of town. Immobilized by shame, my grandmother refused to leave home. In her prayers to Buddha, she indignantly asked The Wise One what she had done wrong to deserve such a daughter. Despite the prayers, my mother's misadventure became the favourite topic amongst idle tongues. As the owner of the trendiest restaurant in town, my mother was an easy target for the tabloids. Anybody who was a somebody knew of her restaurant and name. "Did you hear the new scandal?" people asked each other as if the country was prosperous and politically stable. Social unrest plagued South Vietnam in the early 60s yet Saigon's high society preferred gossiping about an adulteress. The Minister of Foreign Affairs followed my mother's story more closely than he did the country's rocky path. A catastrophic war was about to unfold but nobody could be bothered with the warning signs.

The Minister of Foreign Affairs worked for a repressive regime headed by President Ngo Dinh Diem and his sister-in-law, Mme Nhu. Acting more like a First Lady than a sister-in-law, Mme Nhu enjoyed manipulating the press with her outlandish comments. When her brother-in-law's troops killed dissidents, she described it as the happiest day of her life. When Buddhist monks immolated themselves in protest, Mme Nhu pinched her nose, announcing publicly her distaste for human BBQ. "Let them burn!" she cried. When her sister's marriage faltered, she passed a law forbidding divorces. She travelled the world calling President Kennedy a pinky. Her bitchiness gathered international attention, casting a bad light on South Vietnam. Yet people loved reading about this cute sorceress who came out of nowhere to bewitch the media. But those shenanigans only started in 1963. In 1960, only my mother's sordid tale titillated the Minister of Foreign Affairs.

Handsome Cousin also followed my mother's affairs with a perverted intensity. This handsome lad who fell for my mother's beauty on her wedding day still fantasized about her fifteen years later. When he heard of my mother's restaurant, Handsome Cousin immediately appeared to chat her up. They flirted openly. Her scandalous behaviour only added fire to his yearnings. My mother loved the attention but never took Handsome Cousin seriously. She didn't respect anyone who could sustain a fifteen-year platonic love. Besides, he lacked the bank account my father had.

As a mistress of a man too cowardly to leave his jealous wife, my mother lived through hell. Each new day brought new threats, new harassment, new public humiliation. When the fruit of her illicit activity began kicking inside her womb, my mother knew she had to leave Saigon. She had to hide her shamefully big belly. On a whim, my mother sold her restaurant, severed ties with my father and packed her bags. She traded Saigon's oppressive heat for the cool mountain air of Dalat. Newlyweds came to Dalat for the sweatless lovemaking. Unmarried pregnant women also came to bury their shame in the woods. For protection against beasts of the animal type, my mother brought her brother, my Uncle Hai, with her to Dalat. My mother didn't know it then but in Dalat, another scandal would take place.

Chapter 6

Nam the Ex

The day my cousin Daniel entered the netherworld from a Montreal hospital, Nam, my mother's ex-husband, came out of his coma in another Montreal hospital. Two weeks earlier, Nam had suffered an extensive cerebral hemorrhage after a violent fall in the Métro. Some punks, in their rush to catch the subway train, had pushed the older man aside, causing him to lose his balance, falling head first down a steep flight of stairs. The head trauma brought Nam into a peaceful vegetative state. Brain surgery to drain the cerebral hematoma didn't help. Nam refused to wake up after the five-hour operation. He slept for more than two weeks. Then one day he opened his eyes. A few hours later he started to utter sounds. When he asked for *pho* soup, the family gave a sigh of relief. Miraculously, Nam recovered from an accident that would leave most people comatose for life. Miraculously, he suffered only a right-sided paralysis, a slight speech impediment and a changed mood. Perhaps he would have liked to forget many of the humiliations life had dealt him. But bad luck clung to the old man. Nam came out of his coma with memories intact. And the vivid memories coloured his heart black.

Nam came from a family of hopeless idealists. Their family gatherings consisted of delusional talks of impossible dreams. The siblings fed each other follies no one else took seriously. But, aside from their crazy political chatter, they remained genuinely good souls lost amidst a sea of cheaters, liars and phonies.

"Those American generals are so stupid! How can they win the war? I'll write the CIA to give them advice!"

"No, if I were you, I'd write to Nixon directly!"

"The communists are so stupid too. If I run into Ho Chi Minh, I'd beat the hell out of him for ruining the country!"

My mother could never participate in this kind of conversation. To her, it reeked of nonsense. So she never answered her husband's call. My mother dismissed Nam's words as readily as she rejected his sexual advances. Repulsed by her husband's physique, she couldn't imagine any intimate contact with such a body. When my mother insisted on sleeping alone on their wedding night, Nam respected her wish. When this state of affair continued for months afterward, Nam bit his lips blue. Blue lips and blue balls became a part of his daily life. So the trophy wife, the beautiful, vivacious girl he fell in love with turned out to be nothing more than a sometime sweet but mostly sour apparition. Maybe Nam considered my mother a bitch, but his decency forbade him to express such poison. He could've beaten her up or forced himself on her; Vietnamese men allowed themselves such acts, but he didn't. Unfortunately my mother never appreciated Nam's integrity. She took it as a sign of weakness. She thought of him as a wimp. She saw her husband as a crazy, ugly, spineless man.

My mother's exchange of glances with Handsome Cousin on her wedding day didn't go unnoticed. Unbeknownst to her, Nam caught sight of those furtive signs. The glances gave Nam's heart a quick work over. He palpitated, he flushed, he sweated all at once. It wasn't anger that prevented Nam from swallowing his roast piglet that day. After all, how could he be angry at his innocent younger cousin who committed no crime by looking at the bride? Didn't everyone look at the bride? No, anger didn't wipe the smile from Nam's lips. Jealousy played no part either. It was fear that choked him on his wedding day — the fear of a loveless marriage, the fear of rejection.

Spurned by his new bride, Nam wandered around the countryside for months on end. He took a job as an agricultural engineer. Since this employment required frequent travel, husband and wife were spared each other's silence. During Nam's absence, my mother stayed with her in-laws, sharing a bedroom with Nam's sisters. She never bothered with the whereabouts of her husband. She never wondered if he had mistresses. At fifteen, she preferred daydreaming about impossible love. The reality of war, fixed marriages and unattractive husbands weighed on her pubescent shoulders. But my mother succeeded in forgetting it for a while with mah-jong. To wait out the long hours between gunfire and platonic marital visits, my mother and her sisters-in-law indulged in light gambling.

After years of refusing Nam her body, my mother one day had a change of heart. She decided to have a family. She thought a child would bring happiness to her senseless marriage. A child would keep her mind off Handsome Cousin. A child in time of war would show Fate who's the boss. Seven years after her wedding, my mother finally allowed Nam the forbidden fruit. But if she was still a virgin in fact, my mother was no longer a virgin in thought. Handsome Cousin had ripped her panties off so many times in her fantasy no drop of blood fell to bless the marital bed.

When my brother Tung came into the world in 1952, Nam screamed with ecstasy. He celebrated by wearing a fancy suit. Despite being an heir to a well-off family, Nam always presented himself as an ordinary man. To my mother's disapproval, he'd rather dress in casual pants and flip-flops. Showing off was not his style. Talking politics was more his thing.

Nam adored his first and only son Tung. He spoilt the child with gifts. He showered the kid with attention. He tried his best to raise Tung. But, like most Vietnamese men, he lacked the basic skills. Nam fumbled with diapers. He freaked out when the baby cried. Later, when my brother Tung came home upset because my mother had failed to pick him up from school, Nam spent the afternoon with knots in his guts. His wife's no-show worried Nam. He imagined an accident scenario when in fact a bedroom scene kept my mother away. Unsurprisingly, Nam never suspected my mother's affairs with Buffalo Boy. His imaginary world of political intrigues kept Nam from seeing the truth.

Despite his delusions, Nam understood history. He experienced the spirit of the time more directly than anyone else in our family. In 1975, when we watched the fall of Saigon in our Canadian living room, Nam saw it live on the streets. The chaos outside the American embassy, the last American helicopter to take off from its rooftop, communist tanks rolling into Saigon — Nam witnessed it all on the spot. He felt excited experiencing history first hand. But he also feared an unpredictable future. His only son, my brother Tung, lived thousands of miles away in Canada. Father and son hadn't seen each other since 1970 when Tung left Vietnam with my mother. Nam wondered what Tung was doing the day the communists took over Saigon. Did Tung watch the news footage on TV? Nam missed his son and felt tired all of a sudden.

Nam was named after his motherland, Vietnam. As a patriot unable to control his foolish talk, Nam cultivated enemies. Under the pro-American regime, Nam was tortured for speaking out against "Nixon's stupidity". Accused of being a communist, he spent several months in solitary confinement for this slip of the tongue. Under the communists, he headed back to jail for criticizing "those bunch of Soviets!" In prison, he survived not on brown rice and water but on his idealism. He dreamt of a peaceful, just and independent Vietnam untainted by foreign doctrines. When that dream turned sour in 1975 with the fall of Saigon, Nam kept his crazy man's optimism by building fishing boats. Disillusioned with the new communist regime, Nam joined the exodus of Vietnamese 'boat people'. These people risked their lives fleeing a mass hysteria that turned out to be more benign than moles on a sunburnt back. But who could predict that the Vietnamese communists weren't of Pol Pot's calibre? Unlike Cambodia, no killing fields bloomed in Vietnam, no corpses fertilized rice paddies. But Vietnam in the post-Vietnam War period still remained a place of unrest. Tit-for-tat battles with China and military incursions into Cambodia still denied people peaceful nights. Years after the most important war of the mid-20th century, body bags still filled military trucks. Collective farms and a state controlled economy brought five oranges, three bananas and two tomatoes to the market. People lined up to buy Nothing at their local stores. In the evenings, they went home to watch un-subtitled, un-dubbed revolutionary Russian telecasts. Or they attended communal meetings where everyone pretended to be more communist than the Communists. After a while, people got fed up with the state of things. They wanted out. So they pay a bar of gold each for their boat trip to Freedom, to a Paradise on Earth.

The Boat People saga was not a spontaneous flight toward Democracy, as some would have us believe. The boat trips out of Vietnam were well-organized affairs planned months ahead. Money was exchanged for a place on the boat, diamonds were hidden in bodily orifices to secure a livelihood in the host country, foreign languages were secretly learned to prepare for new lives. Nam knew this scenario by heart. What he didn't know was the locals' sour reaction to his compatriots. South East Asia overflowed with Vietnamese refugees by the early 80s. No one had any appetite for more. Even the big-hearted Christian locals muttered to themselves, "Send this Vietnamese bunch home!" Intact boats carrying healthy passengers devoid of melodramatic tales irked the host governments. There wasn't an official NO TRAGEDY, NO ENTRY policy but some local bigwigs did occasionally take things into their hands.

Nam's boat suffered no major tragedies. When his captain failed to show up at the designated place and time, Nam decided to take over. He had some vague knowledge of boats and this seemed enough to convince the other passengers of his capabilities. Boosted by others' belief in him, Nam became confident. A crazy optimism fuelled him. Despite his inexperience, he felt sure the boat would make it safely to its destination. It was like believing Nixon had read his letters.

Nam's boat ran out of fuel on the second day. Water became scarce on the third day. A midday sun fried some skin while diarrhea affected some colons. But the dehydration didn't cause serious bodily imbalances. A young boy somehow disappeared during the trip. He was one of those kids pushed on the boat by parents too poor to buy spaces for the whole family. One minute the lonely boy sat with hands covering a tearful face. The next minute he vanished. Nobody knew what happened. Preoccupied with their own miseries, no one paid him any attention. Did he swim back to his parents? Did he drown? Except for Nam, nobody cared.

By the beginning of the fourth day, Nam's boat floated toward land. From shore, someone with a loud speaker cried in Vietnamese, "Break your boat! Break your boat or they won't let you land!" This message, at first, confused everyone on board. But they finally understood that there would be no open-arm welcome. In order to land, the refugees would have to do a drowning act first.

Nam's Boat People adventure brought him to Thailand. He became a hero to the people sharing his boat. They worshipped him for getting them safely out of Vietnam. They appreciated his free advice on how to succeed in the West. They didn't think him crazy when he promised he'd write to Ronald Reagan on their behalf. No, they adored Nam and he felt important for the first time in his life.

After a few months in a Thai refugee camp, Nam succeeded in coming to Canada to join our family. In 1983, when my mother laid eyes on her former husband after decades of living separate lives, she felt nothing but pity for him. She only saw him as a poor refugee. She never showed interest in his heroic feat bringing fifty persons to freedom. By this time, my mother had become a successful medical specialist working in Montreal. Her fantasy about fame, recognition and money had come true. In her middle age, my mother only dreamed of a bigger house to impress her rich Westmount colleagues. She dressed in Giorgio Armani suits and drove a Mercedes. The glitz gave her a sense of legitimacy. She no longer felt like the wretched concubine of a married man. Buffalo Boy no longer stirred my mother's desires. The 1960 Dalat scandal no longer kept her sleepless. It still lurked in her subconscious but my mother's busy schedule kept it under lock and key.

In Canada, Nam lived a frugal life. He shared a room with a Vietnamese bipolar woman, finding comfort in her delusions. To save money, she served him canned dog food. To this he would exclaim: "The dog meat in this country is not as tender as back home. It has a strange smell!" He never expected to be fooled by a mental patient. But the bipolar woman didn't intend to deceive Nam. She saw her cousins being fed canned dog food for years in Montreal. She thought, if they all got into McGill medical school, there must be some good in this stuff.

Nam had lost his wife, home, money, country and youthful idealism. But an innate goodness still fuelled him. To keep busy, he spent his days helping new refugees. Versed in French, Nam translated for these lost souls. He brought them to the doctor. He guided them through their Medicare applications. He taught them the subway routes. It was while on one of these volunteer outings that Nam had fallen on his head, pushed by careless passengers.

When Nam came out of his coma, he was a changed man. He no longer laughed. He ceased talking politics. He only answered in monosyllabic phrases. Discharged from the hospital, Nam moved into a chronic-care facility where he spent his old age isolated in a depression no drugs could heal. Eventually Nam stopped speaking completely to live his last years in utter silence.

When Nam died at the age of ninety, my mother felt guilty for the first time in many decades. The affection she denied him throughout his life suddenly made a brief appearance. But it was already too late to ease the suffering. Unfortunately, Nam died a broken man. Till the very end, he remained misunderstood and unappreciated.

Chapter 7

Handsome Cousin

When my cousin Daniel exhaled his last puff of carbon dioxide in a Montreal hospital, Handsome Cousin inhaled truckloads of similar stuff on a congested Parisian boulevard. After decades of dreaming about Paris, Handsome Cousin finally made it to the French capital. Frantically, he asked directions for the *Jardin du Luxembourg*. He had seen photos of the Luxembourg garden years ago in Vietnam and thought it the most romantic place on earth. In his many letters to my mother, Handsome Cousin repeatedly wrote of their future rendezvous at this precise spot. Handsome Cousin felt elated wandering through the famed garden. My mother's absence left a little hole in his spirit but he decided to continue with his quest. He felt her essence in his memory.

A teenaged Handsome Cousin met my mother at her wedding. They crossed paths again five years later at a rice plantation. Fleeing the French vs. Viet Minh bullets in Hanoi, they never expected to see each other alive again. Both giggled at their good fortune at finding safety in the field. While many at the plantation worried about the shortage of food or the fighting in the capital, Handsome Cousin and my mother only worried about covering up their mutual attraction. At the plantation, my mother and her admirer mingled with labourers. She worked the rice paddies while he took care of the farm animals. The physical tasks took their minds off each other. It served as an outlet for their libido. Young and shy, they only dared exchange a few words. "It is hot today, isn't it?" they asked each other every day. They talked of banal things while fragments of unspoken verses danced in their head. When the fighting in Hanoi cooled many months later, my mother and Handsome Cousin reluctantly went their separate ways. They returned to their old homes, to their previous lives, to a time before heartache.

Eight years after the plantation encounter, fate brought these two souls together again in my mother's famous Saigon restaurant. Years of outwitting bullets had toughened their spirits. The timidity of youth had given way to self-confidence. No longer afraid to speak his heart, Handsome Cousin pursued my mother openly. Being the owner of her restaurant, my mother responded with seductive charm, a charm she bestowed on all her clients — males, females and children alike. Handsome Cousin never saw through this. He thought he had special access to Mother's heart. But my father, Buffalo Boy, had beaten him to it. Handsome Cousin spent decades writing my mother passionate letters of longings. She only replied with carefully rehearsed words. Although their paths crossed many times over the years, they were never meant to meet.

When Handsome Cousin learned of my mother's illegitimate pregnancy, he swallowed his pride. Despite everything, he still loved my mother. He wished to offer her and her children a future. When he proposed marriage, my mother answered: "I can't!" But Handsome Cousin persisted. "I have a job offer in Australia. Come with me. Bring the older child. I'll adopt the kid in your belly too. You have no future with a married man! You know he'll never leave his wife!" Once again, my mother shook her head sadly. It wasn't the passion with Buffalo Boy that kept her deaf to such an offer. This passion had cooled quite a bit since the unwanted pregnancy. No, it was my mother's newly found sense of righteousness that kept her from marrying Handsome Cousin. Running off to Australia might sound good but it would only add shame to her family. Imagine running off with the cousin of her ex-husband after being impregnated by her mother's cousin! Wasn't there enough drama?

❦

Four nights before my birth, Handsome Cousin came to see Grandmother in Saigon. Like many others, he had no knowledge of my mother's last-minute hiding place. Handsome Cousin gave Grandmother another 20-page letter addressed to my mother. In it, he pleaded for her to change her mind. His job offer with the Australian Broadcasting Corporation had come through. He would leave for Australia in three weeks. He repeated his marriage proposal. He threatened to stop writing if she didn't answer. Grandmother assured Handsome Cousin she would deliver the letter herself. Of course she didn't. Grandmother unsealed the envelope that very night. Then she read the letter thoroughly. The passion seemed too much for her, so she put it aside for the words to cool. When my mother finally got hold of the letter, six months had passed. Handsome Cousin never knew the fate of his orphaned letter. He left Vietnam with a heavy heart, swearing to never return.

When my mother asked Grandmother about the belated delivery, Grandmother only shrugged. "Oh, I forgot to give it to you!" she replied. For years after that missed appointment with destiny, my mother would wonder about the life she could've had. She could've been a properly married woman living in Australia. I could've had someone to call "Father." Then again, who would be home to take care of Cousin Daniel? Who would carry the weight of her whole family on her shoulders? When I became old enough to understand the complexity of fate (at around age 10), my mother would repeatedly tell me the story of Handsome Cousin. Although she never truly loved him, she felt nostalgic for his court-ship. She promised me we would go to Australia one day to meet him. In her memory, he remained forever the innocent lad loving her the way they only do in 19th century French novels. My mother wanted me to partake of her illusions. And I did with much naiveté. Handsome Cousin became the mythical hero in my fantasies. Although I never met him, Handsome Cousin became the father I would've liked to have had.

Handsome Cousin never married. His teenage obsession for my mother became a lifelong curse. If he couldn't marry her, he didn't want anyone else. In Australia, he worked like a madman to forget the calling of his heart. The Australian Broadcasting Corporation promoted him to Regional Analyst. Commenting on the Vietnam War from the safety of Sydney was an offer he couldn't refuse. So Handsome Cousin devoted all his energy to his job. In private, he led the lonely life of an old bachelor. He only had a couple of friends. He drank and smoked to pass the time away. Years of smoking gave the solitary man emphysema in his old age. On his deathbed, Handsome Cousin asked his Australian friends to find my mother. He had heard she was practicing medicine in Canada. He wanted to send her their old correspondence, which he had kept all these years.

When my mother received her pack of yellowing wrinkled letters along with a note announcing Handsome Cousin's death, she didn't shed a tear. She only said with sadness,

"The poor man!" By that time, my mother was living with a French-Canadian doctor in the northern wilderness of Quebec. Through her Québécois boyfriend, she learned to eat *tourtières*, listen to Felix Leclerc music and played golf. By the mid 80s, my mother had shed the last vestige of her former Vietnamese self. Love, success and good health blessed her new life. Nothing could bring her back to those awful Vietnam years. Not even love letters written by her own young hands.

Chapter 8

Uncle Chinh and Catherine

The day my cousin Daniel died, my heart rhythm went out of sync. But I forced myself to go on. Arrhythmia or not, I had business to take care of. Before dying, Daniel asked me to find his French mother Catherine in France. I was tasked to give her his favourite Cartier ring. Although he hadn't seen his mother in decades, Daniel wanted to give her a proper parting gift. On his deathbed, he felt the need to say: "I forgive you for leaving me."

Finding Catherine in Europe was not hard. I had an old address for her in the south of France, an address clumsily written on a long-forgotten postcard. True to what people say about Europeans not moving, Catherine still lived at the same place two decades later. Cuddled next to her new Italian husband, Catherine couldn't be friendlier. As expected, she shed a couple of tears for Daniel's tragedy. Then she decided to forget her sorrows with a bottle of red wine. Although I had seen old black and white pictures of Catherine taken in Vietnam, I did not recognize her at first. Her dark hair and saucy smile glowed in the photo. Thirty years later, she had become a tired-looking, badly dyed redhead. But the dimples stayed intact. And she wanted to talk. Catherine met my

Uncle Chinh in Paris in 1953. On the fifth anniversary of his brother's execution by French soldiers in Hanoi, Uncle Chinh moved in with his Parisian girlfriend. My family's conflicted loyalty to France never ceased to baffle me. Although I recognized this colonized complex of a people wanting to erase their roots, I could never understand it.

Thanks to his excellent school marks, Uncle Chinh won a scholarship to study in Paris. Airfare, tuition, room and board, all came as a gratuity of the French government. At a time when independence seemed inevitable, no one expected the French colonial authority to send Vietnamese boys to France free of charge. But they did. If the French authority dug mass graves for Vietnamese lads, they also sent planeloads of them to Parisian universities. France's last-ditch effort to brainwash its colonies gave my uncle the time of his life in Paris. While he cursed the French for killing his older brother Tan, my Uncle Chinh thoroughly enjoyed himself in the French capital. His was a contract of deceit signed in hell, but Uncle Chinh was in heaven.

During the day, Uncle Chinh acted the model student in classes. At night, he became another person. To quiet his insatiable libido, he would spend his time cavorting through the Montparnasse district looking for easy French girls. To impress these newly conquered French lasses, Uncle Chinh learned to puff on cigarettes, down red wine and dress like Yves Montand. When Uncle Chinh met Catherine, she was a young hotel maid easily lured by talk of faraway lands. They hit it off right away, falling absolutely in love. Their fairy-tale love knew no constraints — no fixed marriages, no extra-marital affairs, no incestuous liaisons. The relationship would have lasted had it not been for the zeitgeist interfering in their fates.

By 1957, Uncle Chinh had founded a family with his beautiful French maid Catherine. A cute half-breed son named Daniel kept Catherine busy in their small apartment overlooking a noisy street. Although money remained tight, they managed to live correctly. As a graduate of the famed *École Polytechnique*, Uncle Chinh had found a job as second engineer for a local company. He couldn't ask for more.

By 1957, Vietnam's victory over French colonialism had become an event of the past. Although required reading in history classes, this bloody battle for independence left many untouched. Educated Vietnamese still sent their children to French schools where they still sang 'La Marseillaise'. In Saigon's markets, fair-skinned mademoiselles could still shop for French products while their blue-eyed boyfriends still cruised down the boulevard in their Peugeots. Despite the end of colonialism, these untouchables continued their charmed lives, oblivious to the winds of change around them.

By 1957, Vietnam had also witnessed the parting of families as the country split into two. Like many well-off Vietnamese, Uncle Chinh's family had moved south to continue their let-the-maid-take-care-of-it lifestyle. Uncle Chinh's siblings struggled at first but eventually adjusted to their new reality. They succeeded in constructing new lives despite the loss. While Grandmother wallowed in self-pity, her children managed to keep nostalgia at bay. They preferred working. By working hard, my mother became the owner of a trendy restaurant raking in money like they only do in the movies. Optimism floated in the air. A burst of energy pushed people to build, trade, consume. A mass delusion that all was well in South Vietnam kept businessmen rich. Believing in the propaganda fed them by the South Vietnamese government, many people trusted their luck. While the North Vietnamese plotted taking over the South, the South Vietnamese government busied itself with its own agenda: cheat, lie, steal and lie some more.

As a Vietnamese expatriate living in France, Uncle Chinh fell prey to his country's propaganda. The patriotic slogans stirred a sensitive chord in him. It appealed to his pride and sense of nationality. "Isn't it time you come home?" "Come home help us build a new Vietnam!" "We are free of the French, we'll be free of the communists!" "South Vietnam needs your skills! Together we'll build the future!" Like many other expatriate Vietnamese, my Uncle Chinh couldn't resist these words. So he returned to Vietnam. Other compatriots also returned in droves. This mass movement of youthful idealism was not often seen in South Vietnam.

As a reward for his love of the land, Uncle Chinh received the job of chief engineer at Saigon's Waterworks. This made my grandmother very proud. Pride also emanated from her when she set eyes on her beautiful French daughter-in-law. Of course, Grandmother would prefer a humble Vietnamese daughter-in-law obeying her commands to a chain-smoking French woman. But Catherine talked sweetly. And Daniel, the half-breed kid, looked too handsome to leave Grandmother cold. So she spoilt him as much as she did her last son Hai.

Catherine's first few months in Vietnam overflowed with excitement. She enjoyed the attention everyone gave her. She loved having maids at home doing the dirty work while she relaxed at private clubs. As a former Parisian chambermaid, she felt no qualms ordering people around. Oh, how many times had she fantasized about this exact scenario?! At the private clubs, Catherine befriended other French expatriates. Despite the defeat at Dien Bien Phu, many French citizens still called Saigon home. With the addictive taste of colonial life still sweetening their lips, these people balked at the thought of returning to France. In post-colonial Vietnam, they no longer held political power but they still had status as white persons. And their money still went a long way. Back in France, these expatriates would become nobody, another number lining up for unemployment assistance.

At the private clubs, Catherine didn't have to expose herself too long before attracting a horde of French admirers. In Paris, her chambermaid insecurity and cheap clothes overshadowed her beauty. But in Saigon, as wife of the city's chief engineer with nothing to do but pamper herself all day, Catherine glowed. Her dark eyebrows contrasted wonderfully with her light blue eyes. Her ample breasts, glimpsed through light cotton dresses, inspired poems of longings. She became a star at Saigon's private clubs.

When Catherine began acting the diva role entrusted her, my grandmother smelled trouble. Jealousy transformed Uncle Chinh into a mindless monster. If the marriage survived cramped quarters in Paris, it did not survive jealousy fits in Saigon. After a year of marital discord, Catherine packed up her bags to return to France. She didn't make a big scene when my Uncle Chinh insisted on Daniel's custody. "He's my first born son and he stays with me!" Uncle Chinh ordered. "He's a boy, he needs a father figure," Grandmother interjected. "Chinh has a good job here; Daniel will have a better future with his father," said my mother. "We have maids to take care of him, don't worry!" added a teenaged Uncle Hai. Poor Catherine couldn't argue against all these people. Uneducated and unable to speak two words of Vietnamese, Catherine felt powerless against our family. So she left Vietnam with only photos of her beloved Daniel in her suitcase. Daniel, who was only three, and crying *"Maman! Maman!"* non-stop the night his mother took off on an Air France flight.

Chapter 9

Me

The day after Daniel died, Uncle Chinh suffered a massive guilt attack. When Daniel's agony finally left him, we all let out a sigh of relief. Some of us even had wished Death to arrive six months earlier. Uncle Chinh had nurtured such unfatherly thoughts. Visiting Daniel in the hospital pained him. Father and son had little to say to one another. They didn't reminisce about the past. They didn't discuss Daniel's disease. They didn't even argue like in the old days. Daniel's rage prevented him from talking coherently. So he kept silent. The accusatory silence echoed as loudly as the desperate *"Maman! Maman!"* in Uncle Chinh's heart. My uncle wanted to cry but the tears couldn't come.

Two years after Daniel's wailing for his absent French mother, there came another cry for maternal care. In a small rural hospital in Dalat, an unwanted baby, an accident of lust, a product of shame, saw the light of day. I came into this world blue and not breathing yet the attending physician hardly reacted. When the timid cry finally came, the doctor handed me to my mother then left. He acted as if he couldn't care less. Out-of-wedlock babies were better dead than alive. This was the common wisdom in those days. After all, what are a few days of grief if you could spare a lifetime of misery? But despite the lack of good medical care, I survived. And I grew. Being an easy child, I ate all my food. I also slept all night, never got sick and hardly cried. From a blue de-oxygenated newborn I became a quiet, chubby baby cursed with a lazy temperament. My slow-motion reaction exasperated my nimble mother. She forever blamed the obstetrician who de-livered me. "He should've given her oxygen at birth!" she complained every time she saw me struggling at a task. But my mother misread reality. The lack of neonatal oxygen didn't do me in, it was my father's buffalo boy genes that kept me from excelling in school. Like most Oriental moth-ers, she expected me to gather top marks in school then come home to play her a Chopin sonata. When my piano teacher told Mother my tone deafness prevented me from going beyond *'Sur le Pont d'Avignon,'* she gave me a dis-appointed smile. Although my mother loved me, she was never satisfied with me.

Seven years before my disruptive entrance into her life, my mother had a son with her husband Nam. For months she prayed for his birth at the temple. Although not a believ-er, she wanted luck on her side. My mother desired a quick conception, not one that would take month after month of insemination. My brother would be the child to bring hope to Mother's unhappy marriage. Of course, he didn't. He only shouldered a lot of expectations, carrying responsibilities way beyond his age. Despite his parents' strange dynamics, my brother Tung grew up to be an intelligent, well-adjusted young man. When Tung accidentally saw my mother caress-ing Buffalo Boy's neck, he knew better than to report it to his father Nam. Sparing his father the humiliation became more important than healing his own wounded pride. At seven, my brother Tung understood this lesson in life.

For her tryst with my father, my mother had rented a room in her cook's house. Being a Frenchman living in Vietnam but not speaking a word of Vietnamese, the cook stayed immune to gossip. Besides, he didn't care much for the melodramatic carrying on of the Vietnamese. Even if they paid his salary, Vietnamese still stayed Vietnamese. In other words, they did not tickle his curiosity. Fearing recognition by Vietnamese staff at hotels, my mother took refuge at her cook's house. This discreet arrangement suited my parents well. When their grunts exceeded certain limits, the cook would turn on Beethoven Symphony Number Five to mask the sounds of lust. My mother's moans and my father's panting were material for erections, but after a while they got on the cook's nerves. And so began the Beethoven-Buffalo Boy association in my mother's mind. The passion! The passion!

Now in Dalat, with a baby out-of-wedlock on her lap, Mother regretted her beastly acts. She couldn't believe the depth to which her morals had sunk. She felt guilty for cheating on her husband, for letting her son Tung down, for dragging her family's name into the gutter. During those cold Dalat nights, my mother came to her senses. She decided to right her wrongs by doing good. She started volunteer shifts with the nuns. She helped out in the hospital, in the schools. She visited poor people. But in the end, my mother knew her destiny lay in medicine. She would become a doctor like her father. She wanted to return lost pride to her family.

My mother was only fifteen when she had to marry Nam. The war plucked her from her high school class to throw her against a wall of smoke and ignorance. Despite her intelligence, my mother could not finish her secondary school studies on time. Now at thirty, divorced with an unwanted child in tow, my mother vowed to succeed academically. She took correspondence courses and studied at home. She borrowed her brother Hai's school notes to complement her knowledge. She studied hard while I slept on her lap. At the end of the year, she passed her Baccalaureate exams with top-notch scores. At thirty-one, my mother entered Saigon's faculty of medicine as one of only two adult students. She felt ready to return to Saigon with head held high.

My mother often said my birth set her straight. Grandmother on the other hand, blamed me for all that failed in her life. Three months after my birth, my grandfather died of an obvious organic disease. His yellowed skin, bloated stomach and emaciated frame pointed to a physical illness. Given his history of drug addiction, my grandfather probably died of liver disease. But to Grandmother, he died because of Bad Luck. Bad Luck killed my grandfather by poisoning him with her tears of shame. Bad Luck forced my mother into exile, turning a worldly restaurateur into a fugitive hiding behind textbooks. Bad Luck cramped everyone's style when my mother's famous *Aux Délices* restaurant closed. Imagine, no more free pastries for the family. No more job for the French cook. No more meeting place for the Minister of Foreign Affairs. No more illicit sex to the sounds of Beethoven for the Buffalo Boy who grew up to look like an emperor. For many, Bad Luck was a pain in the ass. That Bad Luck, that product of ungodly acts, was no one else but me.

As soon as I grew old enough to make some sense of the world, I understood my role as a bearer of grief in this family. "Life sucks since your birth! " I heard these words so often in my childhood, I mistakenly took them for my nickname. Grandmother felt no remorse throwing her bitterness at me, as if I, a four-year-old, held her destiny in my hands. So I grew up feeling guilty, oh so guilty.

Some of my earliest memories date from 1964. I remember sitting by my grandmother, listening to her stories of family misfortunes. Tales of regrets flowed in the night. But sometimes Grandmother would throw in a bizarre anecdote to test our gullibility. The stories that twisted my mind the most invariably involved food or what passed as delicacies in her days. A regular diet of deep-fried caterpillars did not produce fluttering butterflies in Grandma's gut. Those creatures metamorphosed instead into a meter-long tapeworm tying a knot in her intestine. The dangling thing only saw the light of day, tail first and segment by segment over the course of a week. Although a Buddhist through and through, Grandmother did not hesitate to scream "Hallelujah! Praise the Lord! Finally!" when she saw the tapeworm's severed head performing its last wiggle amidst her stool. While I chuckled over the fate of Grandmother's intestinal parasites, Daniel relished the fantastic tale of a made-in-China coffin. When she turned eighty, Great-Grandmother developed pounding headaches and unrelenting farts for three months. "My mother passed gas three times a day for three months," Grandmother revealed to us one day. With three being an unlucky number, Great-Grandmother thought she heard Death knocking at her door. She convinced her oldest son to buy a sandalwood coffin, which she placed by her bed. She wished to be ready for the other world and she wanted to smell good going there. But the final trip took a long time in coming. Great-Grandmother's sweet-smelling coffin gave out before she did. When her coffin collapsed at her feet, Great-Grandmother gave a shriek. She saw to her horror, rotten cardboard glued to the sandalwood. "My brother ordered that fake coffin from a Chinese crook to save money. When my poor mother saw her son's betrayal, she fell to the floor. Three days after her coffin's demise, she died of a broken-heart attack. The moral to this story? Death can neither be rushed nor delayed. It will come when it will come. Also, never trust your kids and avoid the number three!"

My grandmother loved telling exaggerated tales about her family. She forever reminded us of her glorious past in Hanoi. "Don't forget, I come from a family of mandarins with royal connections. Yes, seven generations of mandarins blessed by the emperors!" Yet when asked how her parents actually earned a living, she replied: "Oh, by making sausages. We had to use our feet to grind the meat!" Although we loved listening to Grandmother's tales, we doubted their veracity. The story about my great-grandmother outliving her coffin amused me. But I knew it must've been a fantasy. Grandmother had lost contact with her own family a long time ago.

When the country split in half in 1954, Grandmother bade farewell to her own mother and brothers. She knew she wouldn't see them again. She made the painful choice of leaving her too-old-to-travel mother behind. While some of Grandmother's siblings joined her in their flight to Saigon, others decided to remain in Hanoi. These were idealistic brothers easily lured by Marxist teachings. Ideologies eventually tore the family apart. Those that stayed behind soon adopted a self-righteous attitude. They went on to fight alongside Ho Chi Minh. They marched for days on empty stomachs through the Ho Chi Minh Trail. In the Cu Chi Tunnel, bringing soldiers from north to south out of sight of the Americans, they crawled through space dug for people fed a lifetime diet of centipedes. Selflessly, these brothers sacrificed their personal lives for the good of the country. Of those siblings who fled south to Saigon, many eventually developed a cynical outlook. They mocked the fanatic beliefs of their brothers back home. But they also felt shame when acknowledging their own beliefs — a belief in the power of money. My grandmother's siblings didn't hate each other but they mistrusted each other. This scenario wasn't unique to our family. It touched thousands of other families. A Berlin

Wall of barbed wire and landmines separated North and South Vietnam in those days. And the Vietnamese Iron Curtain seemed just as sinister as that of Eastern Europe.

Once you left, there was no turning back. Communication remained impossible between the two Vietnams. Neither letters nor phone calls could be exchanged. For thirty years, my grandmother lost contact with her family in Hanoi. For thirty years, she dreamed of returning to her mother's home. But such reverie remained impossible. All her life, my grandmother would be haunted by dreams of her aging mother. All her life, Grandmother would regret leaving her own mother behind. The story of Great-Grandmother outliving her coffin was probably Grandmother's guilt talking to her at night.

My grandmother's sessions of oral history fascinated my cousin Daniel and me. So, while my brothers Tung and Tim tinkered with their machines, Daniel and I gathered around Grandmother's dried up feet to better catch her words. We wanted to be our family's storytellers when we grew up. "If we grow up," we told each other. Even as kids, we understood the dangers of the war around us.

By the mid 1960s, the American involvement in the Vietnam War had reached its point of no return. Thousands of American soldiers had already lost their innocence in the jungle's booby traps but President Lyndon Johnson, believing the war to be winnable, pledged more troops and more money. A large part of that money did go into building infrastructure and buying equipment for the South Vietnamese Army fighting their brothers in the North. But a good part also went straight into the pockets of corrupt South Vietnamese generals. The more money the Americans spent on Vietnam, the more their allies in the South Vietnamese Army died. There seemed to be a direct inverse relationship. Yet no one wondered why. No one noticed that, as the generals grew richer and fatter, they became less interested in the war. Their only strategic planning was to build mansions for their mistresses behind their wives' backs.

In our neighbourhood, we saw more widowed mothers, more children suddenly left fatherless. The sounds of funeral gongs and rented weepers become a bothersome weekly ritual keeping us awake in the evening. Funeral processions were once elaborate, colourful affairs. But by the mid-60s funerals had become expedited events. No one had any appetite for repetitive mourning on our street. So they hired professional weepers for the job. Death lost its magic touch on us children. It became real and immediate but not yet banal.

The war took a dangerous turn in 1968. On the eve of *Tet*, the Vietnamese New Year, the communists launched a surprise attack on the South. With many soldiers away on holiday, the unprotected cities of South Vietnam toppled like dominoes. Even the American embassy in Saigon fell into communist hands for more than a week. While many cities burned, the imperial city of Hue suffered the most damage. The fighting reduced many of Hue's priceless historical monuments into forlorn rubble. Civilian casualties amounted to the tens of thousands. The American, North Vietnamese and South Vietnamese armies all suffered heavy losses.

My Horny Uncle Hai spent those dangerous months in the front line. Although I detested his macho behaviour, I prayed for him every evening. The whole family spent restless nights worrying for his safety. Unfortunately for him, Uncle Hai was the only male in the family young enough to be drafted into an army on the verge of losing the war. Actually, Uncle Hai never tasted the fear of bullets. As the battalion's doctor, he was spared direct contact with enemy fire. He didn't shoot. He only collected maimed bodies, stitched them, bandaged them or splinted them. He put into practice what he had learned in medical school — cleaning wounds, then using antibiotics to prevent gangrene. With this simple procedure, my uncle saved those who had seemed hopeless. Out of 10 casualties, six would live under his hands. He soon became known as Doctor 6-10. This was a much better title than the old Doctor 4-10 of previous years. Thus, my uncle became a hero to his comrades in arms. When Uncle Hai returned to Saigon a decorated sergeant, we all beamed with pride. My uncle gave a wide grin when he greeted Grandmother. Yet he never said much about his experience on the front. We only heard of his fear going to the outhouse at night. "Nobody wanted to go outside at night. So we all pissed in our helmets."

The battle of *Tet* '68 destroyed my relatives' homes. With all their worldly possession up in smoke, some of my aunts and uncles moved in with us. Having so many people at the dinner table put excitement in our life. It later became a drag listening to their lectures. They all took on the bossy parental role without being asked.

When Saigon burned under communist rockets in '68, my mother decided to take shelter in the garage. We moved from a third floor apartment to a main floor garage. Somehow we felt secure having two floors of cement above our heads. Just to be on the safe side, we also prayed for the rockets to stop their destruction in mid-flight. We prayed cross-culturally — I to Jesus and my grandmother to Buddha. Squeezing the whole extended family into a windowless one-car garage was no small feat. Rats nibbled at our feet at night while cockroaches scurried across our arms. We slept on straw mats placed directly on a cement floor still smelling of diesel oil. We suffered from the oppressive heat and the indignity of sharing our farts with twelve other family members. The lack of oxygen turned our dreams into deliriums.

On one of those unbearable nights, I felt a large rat crawling up my left thigh. As I tried shooing it away, I realized it ran on five bony fingers. I froze with fear as I remembered ghostly tales of dead hands coming alive at night. Grandmother used to scare me with those eerie war stories — how blown up hands returned to reclaim a bit of the marital bed for themselves. No longer able to control my fear, I cried out. Just as immediately, the bony hand retreated. Nobody asked me the reason for my outburst. They just said: "Mai, go to sleep!" The bony hand reappeared a few days later on my stomach. It tried groping inside my pyjama pants. When I finally gathered enough courage to scream "hand of the ghost!" my mother answered: "Mai, you're dreaming! Now be quiet or else ..." Once again, the ghostly limb disappeared with my second scream. On the third occasion, the bony hand managed to slip inside my underwear, digging into my vagina. No longer able to tolerate the prickling sensation of newly chewed nails on my skin, I shouted, "There's a hand inside my underwear!" With those words, the bony hand vanished in a flash. It never returned to haunt me after that third episode. The wandering hand feared being named. It dreaded being unmasked, working best in the darkness of the night. Yet it also enjoyed the risk of being exposed. Perversely, it fantasized about being caught in the act by others.

❧

The local media went wild with the battles of *Tet* 1968. Night after night, death and destruction came to haunt us in grainy black and white. "Look what the communists did!" "The communists destroyed the imperial city of Hue!" "They massacred civilians!" "There are mass graves around Hue!" With television bombarding us with these announcements, we soon fell prey to their hate messages. Our ancestral city of Hanoi soon morphed into a pariah state and Ho Chi Minh inevitably became our Public Enemy Number One. It was only much later, as an adult in Canada, that I saw news footage of American planes bombing Hanoi, of Agent Orange being sprayed on North Vietnamese forests, of American napalm scorching innocent children, of a mass massacre of civilians at My Lai. As a child growing up in South Vietnam, I knew nothing of these facts of history. Brainwashed, I stayed blind to the North Vietnamese's suffering. Yet they were also my people. And they suffered so much more than we did.

Years later, I also learned how the events of *Tet* '68 influenced the world. In France, violent anti-war protests paralyzed Paris for weeks. May '68 became a rallying cry for young Parisians. Decades after this mass protest, future French presidents still boast of their participation in the event. "Where were you in May '68?" became a question many future politicians would trip over. In North America, the anti-war movement gave rise not only to civil disobedience, it also unleashed a wave of creativity. John Lennon wrote *Revolution* in '68 and later bared his bum to the public in a Montreal hotel room. In Germany, radical students even took up arms for the Vietnamese cause. Perversely, they killed bourgeois Germans in the name of oppressed Vietnamese peasants. Japan, known for its respect for law and order, also saw violent anti-war protesters ruining cherry blossom festivals. Growing up in South Vietnam, I had no awareness of this. The friendly American soldiers giving me candies on the streets were in fact Public Enemy Number One on the world's stage. Yet the mainstream South Vietnamese media, in total denial, never let out a peep. It was *Life* magazine that taught me the history of my country.

❧

My mother changed after the battles of *Tet* '68. She no longer cared for illicit affairs and useless love letters. The capture of the American embassy showed her how vulnerable life could be. If the American embassy was not safe, how could we be safe? From that day on, my mother became obsessed with one idea: to leave Vietnam. To leave Vietnam before things deteriorated further.

Despite the war, life went on as usual in my school. In those days, I attended a private Catholic school, not for the religion but for the strict upbringing. Unlike my grandmother, my mother didn't believe in God. She just wanted me in the proper mould early. She feared I would run wild like she once did. So a traditional Catholic school suited her just fine. In school, the nuns taught us arithmetic and embroidery. We learned to read and to pray. We even had music classes. Not once did the nuns discuss the war. Not even when classmates' fathers perished on the battlefields. Not once did we learn any useful survival skills. The nuns carried on as if God walked on their side, as if the war could never be lost.

When fathers of classmates died, I didn't feel bad for them. I felt jealous instead. My mourning friends came to school bragging about the heroic deeds of their fathers. "My father did this. My father did that," became standard talk in the schoolyard. The girls wanted to outdo each other with their tales of family grief. Having no father, I kept quiet about mine. How I would've liked my father to die a heroic death too. But he lived and was still spreading his semen around indiscriminately. Naturally I couldn't tell any of these dirty secrets to my classmates. So I invented stories about a father that never existed.

I saw my father twelve times during my whole child-hood. He preferred short afternoon rendezvous to lengthy evening ones. We all knew he came for my mother's embrace, not for me. During these visits, he'd lavish her with extravagant gifts. He didn't bring one bottle of champagne — he brought a whole case. Despite her resolution to end the relationship, my mother sometimes gave in to the call of my father's flesh. With their secret affair exposed, they no longer needed to hide. Without her ex-husband in the house, my mother felt free to bring her lover home. My parents made quick love while my grandmother and brothers napped in the room next door. They thought they were safe from prying eyes, but Daniel and I, we saw it all through the keyhole.

I didn't hate my father. I only felt indifference for this person whose contribution to my life amounted to a random sperm. Somehow, I had more affection for Nam, my mother's ex-husband. He, too, visited us occasionally. But Nam couldn't share my mother's bed. He only shared my grandmother's tea on those visits. Nam could've resented me, the product of his ex-wife's illicit love. But his decency wouldn't allow him such sentiments. He treated me as his child although we weren't related. I called him Uncle Nam while my father stayed 'Buffalo Boy' to me. When my father died in 1984, I was living in Montreal. I heard of the death two years after the fact. In Canada, my father and I became complete strangers although we shared the same city. He moved there four years after we did. With his many contacts at the Foreign Affairs Ministry, my father managed to obtain an exit visa a few weeks before the fall of Saigon. In Montreal, he didn't contact me and I had no urge to see him. We would have nothing to say to each other if we did meet. Years later, I found out he had another 'favourite' mistress after my mother left him. On his deathbed, he asked for this mistress. Instead of throwing a jealous fit, his wife obediently waited for the mistress' tearful arrival before closing the coffin. Even in death, Buffalo Boy seduced women.

⁓

Grandmother told us many family stories but she never bothered explaining who was who. An aunt here, an uncle there, yet we never knew their names. What if she forgot the truth and invented half those tales? That, we could never be sure of. But the tales entertained us so we listened to them in earnest. Each night after dinner we would gather around Grandmother. We wanted to be close enough to hear her soft voice, but also far enough to avoid her line of spit. Daniel and I constantly fought for the right spot around Grand-mother's dried-prune feet.

Younger, I couldn't remember any story about Horny Uncle Hai fathering my brother Tim. This was the bomb that my grandmother successfully hid from us all these years. I discovered that scandal by chance only at the ripe age of 26. Shock more than shame kept me from divulging the secret to Tim. But I did share the story with my cousin Daniel. Daniel and I always shared stories.

Chapter 10

My Cousin Daniel

The night my cousin Daniel passed away, his favourite nurse stayed home. Although she promised to guide him down the end of the road, that accompaniment never took place. Unfortunately, Daniel's end of the road moment occurred during Anne's day off. Nurse Anne normally kept a healthy distance from her patients. But she couldn't resist my cousin Daniel's stories. She'd never heard so many exaggerated tales belonging to the same family. She thought Daniel invented them all until she remembered morphine made you sleepy, not creative.

Only Nurse Anne sat with Daniel during his last few days on earth. Our family could no longer stomach the sight of his hallow eyes, distorted face and emaciated frame. Daniel asked me once to pour lotion on his legs to relieve the itchiness of his dry, leathery skin. While I dreaded touching him with my naked hands, I feared even more hurting his feelings by wearing gloves. So I massaged him with the tips of my fingernails, which I immediately clipped off once home. Eventually, I took the cowardly way out — I stopped visiting him in the hospital. One by one we ceased coming. We let the nurses do their dirty jobs and, for that, thanked them with boxes of Belgian chocolates. Perhaps Nurse Anne harboured more resentment toward us than Daniel did. He had given up on us long ago.

Even as I avoided Daniel, I thought about him night and day. In my spare time, I scoured the dubious shops of Montreal's Chinatown for a miracle cure. Rhinoceros horns? Seahorse tails? Bear claws? Fish bladder stew? "No, all that stuff is for old sicknesses," said the famous Dr Tan of La Gauchetière Street. "This is a new sickness. We don't know what to do with it either. Try meditation." This quack doctor's office overflowed with patients coming from the four corners of the country. They all swore by his grasshopper and silkworm brews. But for my cousin Daniel, Dr. Tan's insectariums offered no relief. To give Daniel some hope, I bought him how-to-books on self-hypnotism, visualization techniques and positive thinking. I had read somewhere that gold-medal athletes actively visualize the final leap that will break world records months before starting to train. And if visualization can give results in sport, why can't it offer hope in medicine? In those days, my mother's *New England Journal of Medicine* only reported statistics. How many died this year compared to last year? How does the US death rate compare with that of Africa? What is the ratio of male to female mortality? Numbers filled our heads. Hope escaped our hearts. Since viral modes of transmission remained a mystery for researchers, treatment stayed impossibly out of reach for clinicians. And instead of blaming doctors for their helplessness, we blamed the patients for their ungodly lifestyle. We blamed and we never forgave.

Naturally my Uncle Chinh reacted with shock when he discovered his son Daniel's disease. "HIV and AIDS?" he grasped. Like my grandmother, Uncle Chinh never accepted Daniel's homosexuality. As a womanizer, Uncle Chinh couldn't imagine having a son who preferred penises to voluptuous breasts. The day Uncle Chinh learned of Daniel's diagnosis, he decided to phone his son for a man-to-man talk. But he couldn't get his words out, he couldn't acknowledge the truth. "Are you OK? I heard you have hemorrhoids," he said. Like my grandmother, Uncle Chinh could only talk in code. Hemorrhoids stood for both homosexuality and the shameful disease that went with it. Uncle Chinh knew of our family's curse. We had endured too much to blame it on chance alone. My Uncle Tan facing the French firing squad in Hanoi, my grandfather's opium addiction, the family's loss of fortune during Vietnam's partition, my mother playing concubine to her third cousin, the deadly Vietnam War that killed so many of our friends, the Boat People saga. Those were Vietnamese curses Uncle Chinh managed to digest. But homosexuality and AIDS? My uncle could not understand these Western curses.

"Well, Daniel's mother is a French woman," my grandmother reminded Uncle Chinh. "You married her, remember? That explains the Occidental curse!" Then, she quickly added: "No homosexuality in my Vietnamese family. Don't know what it is and never heard of it!" Grandmother loved dismissing things. She also enjoyed criticizing others. Naturally, she never blamed herself, never questioned her own actions. If Daniel turned out blemished, Grandmother pointed her finger elsewhere. In Grandmother's mind, Daniel's problems stemmed from Catherine's basement bargain genes. These French genes that gave birth to a randy narcissist weren't of the Champs Élysées quality. They were more likely something out of the Paris catacombs.

Daniel's feeling for his mother Catherine remained a mystery to me. It stayed forbidden territory for both of us. Yes, Daniel took pride in the French genes that gave him a whiter complexion, taller stature, a more refined nose. But he also sneered at Catherine's chambermaid background.

He could go for years without ever mentioning her name. On the rare occasion when he did refer to his mother, it would be either "the stupid fool" or "that beautiful woman". Catherine became a paradox for both of us. We thought we knew her but we knew we didn't.

If Daniel's feelings for his mother stayed ambiguous, his passion for his lovers wasn't. He loved them all. He loved to make them salivate as he danced about naked, whistling a Lou Reed tune. Daniel's list of lovers would put Horny Uncle Hai's to shame. My French cousin started seducing teachers at the ripe age of 14. His effeminate face on a hairless torso left straight men perplexed. Many of these men went to sleep with questions in their hearts then woke with a strange midnight thirst no water could quench. Daniel had no qualms about bedding married men. He didn't mind sleeping with his friends' fiancés. He could also lure American GIs away from female prostitutes in Vietnam. No, Daniel never slept for money. He did it for the addictive feeling of being wanted. To compensate for an absent mother, he hosted penises in his rectum.

As a mixed breed, Daniel looked beautifully exotic. Heads turned wherever he ventured and he did venture to many places. From Montreal's constipated literary world to Paris' seedy saunas, from Munich's prestigious ballet scene to Maui's nudist beaches, from Key West's hippie bars to Provincetown's trendiest boutiques — Daniel wowed them all with his looks and talent. His piano recitals brought chills to listeners. His funky handmade dresses sold like hot cakes in Provincetown. His faultless accent in five languages made people wonder just where the hell is this guy from? Italy? France? Germany? Canada? Vietnam? Nooo! Can't be Vietnam!

At those Provincetown beach orgies where love was supposedly anonymous, Daniel was always sought out for his muscle squeezing ability. Uncle Hai's videos of Thai prostitutes puffing cigarettes with their vaginas left a deep impression on a young Daniel. We found and watched those videos together in stunned silence one day. Inspired, my cousin spent his youth practicing this manoeuvre using his other orifice. As with everything else he did, Daniel excelled at this craft.

Provincetown smelled of sex in the late 70s. The odour of sperm, saliva, vaginal juices permeated the washrooms of its bars. The town's salty air turned people wild with sexual thirst. The sun liberated their libido and facilitated casual encounters of the flesh. Young homosexuals, heterosexuals, bisexuals all craved an exchange of bodily fluids. My cousin Daniel spent one summer working in Provincetown. He was a haughty maitre d' in a French restaurant at night. During the day, he ran a boutique selling avant-garde dresses. On his days off, he became a wild beast engaging in beach orgies. He fucked as if there would be no tomorrow. And a lowly virus entered his bloodstream that summer in Provincetown.

The way Daniel toyed with his numerous identities impressed me. His sexuality seemed just as fluid. Male, female, what did it matter? He played well the chameleon role, getting a kick out of deceiving people. Yes, my cousin Daniel lied unabashedly. He mastered the sport of infidelity. He also shoplifted for fun and snorted coke in exchange for stolen kisses. Yet to Grandmother, Daniel remained her handsome wholesome French pianist. Up till the very end, Daniel managed to fool my grandmother with his sweet talk. He lived like a spy with two, three, four parallel lives. Unfortunately, he wasn't prepped for his final role — that of a fatally ill 30-year-old man.

Daniel's sickness was swift. Yet it also lingered on. The virus took 22 months to multiply, spread and do its job. Daniel spent the first three months in denial. Then he entered magical thinking mode. He thought his trip to Dubrovnik the summer before might save him. That year Chernobyl made headlines with its nuclear reactor explosion. In Daniel's mind, Dubrovnik seemed close enough to Chernobyl to shower him with a decent dose of radiation. "And if radiation kills men, it kills viruses too, doesn't it?" Daniel's delusions stretched far in those days.

Before he reached his last stage of morphine-induced stupor, Daniel experienced days of rage. Except for a few of us, he hated everyone in our family. He'd often call me to bitch on "that lowly dog of a man" — his father. He blamed Uncle Chinh for keeping him in Vietnam when his mother Catherine returned to France. He blamed Catherine for not trying harder to take him away. My cousin's custody decision had been a matter of convenience. It freed Catherine from the duties of motherhood. It also satisfied his father's traditional belief that a first-born son belongs to the groom's family. In all this business of divorce and parting, nobody thought of Daniel's well-being.

After Catherine's departure, Uncle Chinh doted on Daniel. He bought my cousin all kinds of toys. He took him out for ice cream every Sunday while the rest of us kids drooled. This period lasted about three years. Harsh discipline accompanied by a form of indifference came next. As a good-looking divorced man, Uncle Chinh didn't stay celibate for long. Vietnamese ladies soon filled his nights. He married one of those Vietnamese ladies, eventually forgetting his fatherly duties. In France, Catherine also remarried and bore another child. So her monthly words of affection to Daniel slowly dried up. By the late 60s, her postcards from France ceased to arrive. Sadly, Daniel became a ward of the Vu family at the age of 10. The adults in our family shared responsibilities for him. But with the Vietnam War and other worries on our hands, no one really cared.

Reflecting on his youth filled Daniel with hatred. Days in bed with nothing to do helped Daniel see what he spent his whole life repressing. So he vowed to take revenge. Being the keeper of our family's secrets, he had immense power. Daniel could undo a generation of hypocrisy with a few simple stories. And he felt ready to spread the word.

Chapter 11

My $99 Special

A few months before dying, Daniel asked to see my Provincetown scrapbook. He wanted to view again images from that careless summer before paranoia transformed our lust into fear. As I leafed through my scrapbook, an old Greyhound bus pass caught my eye. "$99 Thank You Canada Special," it said in the back. With a smile, I showed the bus pass to Daniel. When my cousin shrugged in confusion, I reminded him of our summer in Provincetown.

"Do you remember it? I took the bus to see you that summer. It was 1980."

"The Thank You Canada summer?" Daniel asked, suddenly remembering facts half forgotten.

Yes, a Thank You Canada summer when Canadians actually registered a blip on their southern neighbours' radars. The previous year, hostile Iranians had stormed the American embassy in Teheran, taking many hostages. Daily chants of "Death to America!" sent shivers down people's spines. Ken Taylor, our Canadian ambassador in Iran, swiftly acted by providing six American diplomats with fake Canadian passports. He saved them from the 444 days of captivity their compatriots went through. When this story hit the newsstands, Americans reacted with an outpouring of love. The maple leaf flew in many American front yards. Motels offered specials to Canadians. Restaurants accepted the Canadian dollar at par. Greyhound introduced the $99 Thank You Canada pass. All this capitalist benevolence tempted me. So I bought my Greyhound ticket, determined to re-visit the USA of my nightmares.

Before landing in Provincetown, where Daniel ran a small clothing store, I headed south to Key West. The thirty-six-hour bus ride to Florida opened my eyes to the despair of coloured people. I thought Vietnamese had it bad until I witnessed extreme poverty in one of the world's richest countries. At bus stations, I saw homeless people rummaging through garbage while their hungry dogs lapped up toilet bowl water. On treeless sidewalks, I took photos of men sleeping on cardboard beds then felt guilty for owning a big Nikon. While there were many snapshots of gloom, my photos also showed images of natural beauty, architectural marvels and smiling people, both black and white. This first big trip alone intoxicated me.

With the Vietnam War long over, people no longer saw me as a Viet Cong threat on the streets of small town America. By 1980, the communist menace, although still present, had taken second stage to the new Muslim challenge. That challenge would transform into a catastrophe in the next decades; but in 1980, it was still only a struggle between "us and some fanatic Iranians."

The early 80s also saw the exodus of innumerable Vietnamese Boat People. After tragic accidents at sea or an interminable stay in overcrowded refugee camps, many of these people eventually settled in Europe, Australia, North America. While some joined illegal gangs or stayed for an eternity on social welfare, most managed to build new lives. Their children succeeded academically, entering medical schools in droves. Their hard work earned them lifestyle stories in local newspapers. As minor characters, the Boat People become popular in urban novels and television shows. Even children's books started featuring a 'Kim' or a 'Lan'. Like dandelions, *'pho'* restaurants popped up in almost every city centre across North America. When the *New York Times* devoted a whole section to this Vietnamese food staple, the Boat People knew their moment of fame had come. It was now cool to be Vietnamese. Doubly cool to be a Vietnamese-Canadian.

Provincetown, Massachusetts in 1980 shared none of Derby, Connecticut's stifled small town air. If my Derby classmates excluded me from their games in 1970, if they teased my accent and called me names in school, if they pushed me around and covered my locker with nasty words, their Provincetown compatriots did all they could to compensate for this lonely period. In Provincetown, I metamorphosed into an exotic-looking Canadian, a Canadian who spoke three languages, who at 20, had lived while many merely played at make believe. Would-be artists sought me out to chat, to flirt, to feel my naturally hairless legs.

The summer I came to Provincetown, Daniel had just broken up with his latest boyfriend. To keep busy, my cousin indulged in other men. He also spent time obsessively designing outlandish costumes for his boutique. His creativity kept him floating on a permanent high. I never saw him crying over ex-lovers. My summer in Provincetown was supposed to last one week. It stretched over three months. I stayed to help Daniel mind his store. I also stayed to purge my heart of poison.

Although he didn't pay me, I liked working in his boutique. A toilet, hotplate and mattress in the back of the store became my living quarters. I survived on one-dollar tacos or the occasional second-hand steak Daniel brought back from his restaurant job. On tight days, I would go searching for mussels on the beach. If all else failed, I knew where to find free Hare Krishna lentil soups. Despite the tight financial situation, I loved the sensation of freedom, of carelessness. I followed in Daniel's footsteps, entertaining boys on my mattress. I let alcohol lubricate my spirit. I giggled when lovers compared my breasts to bite-sized cupcakes. They laughed when I nicknamed their penises 'anacondas'. For one brief summer, I forgot all about a bony hand digging into my underwear at night, about a long-ago war, about my absent father, about the bullies in Derby, Connecticut, about my uninspiring studies at McGill regurgitating chemical formulas to please my family.

While I experimented with sex, I did so with much caution. Being a child out of wedlock, I understood the consequences of careless encounters. I knew another unwanted pregnancy in the family would kill Grandmother. So I protected myself. Daniel on the other hand never felt the need for protection. As a healthy young man, he felt invincible. Besides, who'd wear condoms at beach orgies?? The syphilis-gonorrhoea-chlamydia cocktail hardly dented my cousin's libido. He knew where to get antibiotics. Ugly genital warts sprouting everywhere? Leave it to liquid podophyllin for a thorough job. Why, there is a cure for everything, he thought naively. Unfortunately for Daniel, the virus that would eventually kill him still carried no name in 1980.

That summer in Provincetown changed both of us forever. Liberated from the haunting of old ghosts, I returned to McGill determined to switch from biochemistry to psychology. For a few brief weeks in Provincetown, I saw the darkness in my soul giving way to laughter. Intrigued, I wanted to better understand this process, to study this transformation in myself and in others. Daniel also returned to Montreal after our summer in Provincetown. Back home, he moved in with a new lover — a writer who promised to tell his tale to the world. Daniel giggled at this promise. "Don't forget my grandmother's stories of tapeworms and a made-in-China coffin!" he said. "My family is royally screwed up. There are lots of perverted tales and there'll be lots more to come!" Little did Daniel know that his life story would end a few years after that summer in Provincetown.

Chapter 12

Aunt Thu and the Pedophile

My cousin Daniel died alone one Thursday afternoon. The first person to be notified of this death was Horny Uncle Hai. Being both a family member and a family doctor to Daniel, he was naturally the first one the nurse called. Besides, Daniel's own father refused to pick up the phone. Still in denial, Uncle Chinh could not understand how and when hemorrhoids had become lethal.

Upon receiving the sad but expected news, Uncle Hai repeatedly thanked Nurse Anne. He had noticed the angle of her upturned breasts the week before so he wanted to be on her good side. At home, no longer able to rein in his emotions, Uncle Hai turned dark. He hurled insults at his girlfriend. "You're fat! Stop eating!" he'd scream over and over. Then he cried. It could've been the tears of a physician unable to cure his patient. Or it could've been the tears of a young boy not able to fix his broken life. And the memory of that impotence would stay with my uncle forever.

When Grandfather died in 1960, Uncle Hai had barely reached adulthood. Being the baby in the family, my uncle suffered the most. While his older siblings, too busy with their own families, dried their tears in due time, Uncle Hai couldn't stop the flow of his. His beloved father, an important doctor in his time, had entered the other world a lowly drug addict betrayed by his liver. The image of an emaciated, yellowed skeleton would haunt Uncle Hai for many years.

While Good Fortune held Uncle Hai's left hand, Bad Fate pulled his right arm. Despite his spoiled-brat childhood, my uncle also fell victim to life's vicissitudes. The war of independence against the French left its mark on a young Uncle Hai. In 1948, during the worst months of this conflict, Uncle Hai left home for the safety of the countryside. This flight to safer ground was done on foot and without parental guidance. "You children go with your older sister Thu. I'll stay home to take care of the house and your ailing father," Grandmother insisted despite Uncle Hai's cries. Aunt Thu accepted this last-minute command as passively as she accepted her fixed marriage at seventeen. After 10 minutes of preparation, Aunt Thu became reluctant surrogate mother to her three youngest siblings: Uncle Hai, Aunt Shirley and Uncle Chinh.

&

Aunt Thu was Grandmother's second child. Her seriousness set her apart from her siblings. She excelled in school, collecting academic awards as easily as one collected seashells. Naturally, Aunt Thu earned her teachers' love. Long after her graduation, they all remembered her quick wit and thin lips uttering words way beyond her age. French teachers, who normally wouldn't socialize with Vietnamese students outside of school, waved to Aunt Thu on the streets. They'd even approach my aunt, introduce themselves to my grandmother to congratulate her for bearing such a gifted child. Of course, Grandmother beamed with pride.

Of all the teachers met by chance on the streets, Grandmother liked Mlle Caillot the most. She was a young, soft-spoken woman with baby blue eyes. She always wore a nondescript brown suit but Grandmother did notice a large golden cross dangling from a chain around her neck. When Grandmother met Mlle Caillot for the first time in 1945, she didn't expect to cross paths with her again three years later in a hospital ward. But fate has funny ways of doing things. In 1948, Grandmother did run into Mlle Caillot again. The French teacher volunteered for the Red Cross that year. "Yes, French soldiers brought your husband, Dr. Vu, to the hospital. He spoke perfect French so the soldiers thought he was on our side. He's now living with one of your relatives." Those three French sentences buoyed Grandmother's spirit. They gave direction in her search for lost family members. Thanks to them, she did find her husband. After that episode, Aunt Thu became a diamond in her parents' eyes.

❧

All her life, my mother would compare herself to her older sister, Thu. Because Aunt Thu breezed through her teacher's-pet role, she naturally received more parental praise. My mother, on the other hand, only heard "hummmpphhh!" for her efforts. This lack of parental acknowledgement would haunt my mother for the rest of her life. To earn her parents' attention, my mother took on her shoulders responsibilities reserved for others. Without being asked, she would sometimes assume the maid's chores by scrubbing the floor. When my grandfather exchanged opium for morphine, my mother offered to search for morphine on the streets. When the morphine plugged his bowels, she volunteered to give her father an enema. But in my mother's mind, Thu remained the preferred daughter.

While my mother envied Aunt Thu her intelligence, my aunt lost sleep dreaming of Mother's lifestyle. Aunt Thu craved Mother's scandalous nights and steamy afternoons. Secretly, Aunt Thu wished to follow my mother's footsteps, to break the conventions of society, to walk out on a fixed marriage, to leave a man she didn't love. But she didn't dare do it. Despite her intelligence, Aunt Thu lacked courage.

While my mother lived a carefree life, Aunt Thu remained a serious young woman committed to her studies. While young men flocked to my mother, they steered clear of Aunt Thu. Soon a rivalry developed between the two sisters, a rivalry both felt but would not acknowledge.

❧

Like my mother, Aunt Thu entered into a pre-arranged marriage while still a teenager. The groom, a frail and cowardly looking man, came from a family of intellectuals. His thinning hair left my aunt lukewarm but his family pedigree impressed her. As the son of a scholar, the groom never learned any useful skills. He was incapable of doing anything besides teaching mathematics and taking photos. His helplessness fed his domination over my aunt. "Thu, can you do this?" "Thu, do that for me!" Aunt Thu never complained. She obeyed his every command with her usual answer "Yes, my Other Half!" Her lifelong loyalty to her husband perplexed our family. We wondered if she really cared for him. Or did she only follow the Confucian dictum to the letter "Obey your spouse like you obey your parents!" At family reunions, Aunt Thu's husband never spoke much. His lack of words cast a spell on us. Grandmother saw it as the silence of the wise. In fact, it was the silence of a perverted mind ruminating forbidden things.

In 1948, Aunt Thu played surrogate mother to her three youngest siblings. My grandmother's order couldn't be any clearer: "Thu, you bring the three youngest ones to safety. Hanoi is too dangerous, you must get out! Go to Thai Binh village, it's safer there. Hai's still a baby. Carry him if he gets tired. Shirley's stupid. Make sure she doesn't do dumb things. Chinh should be alright. Now go!" Aunt Thu's husband disapproved of this arrangement but only ground his teeth. Fearing both the French and the Viet Minh rebels, he wanted to be as invisible as possible. Their night escape to the countryside had to be a quiet affair. Having a bunch of kids cramped his style. But he didn't argue. True to his quiet nature, he didn't say much. For hours, Aunt Thu, her family and friends hid under a bridge while the footsteps of French soldiers thundered overhead. When all seemed clear, they continued on, crossing field after muddy field. Everyone took turns carrying a tired Uncle Hai and a tired Kim, Aunt Thu's son.

Two days later, when they arrived at Thai Binh village, Aunt Thu headed straight for the famous Nguyen plantation. The rice plantation belonged to Nam, my mother's husband. Being of a generous nature, Nam opened the plantation to all friends and relatives. He welcomed anyone seeking refuge from war-torn Hanoi. His plantation offered peace and decent food. It also reeked of forbidden love.

After pulling the last leech from her siblings' legs, Aunt Thu let out a loud sigh of relief. She had kept her promise to Grandmother. They were now safe and sound. Aunt Thu gave another sign of relief when she saw my mother in the kitchen the next day. The sisters had left bullet-ridden Hanoi on different days, taking different routes. They weren't sure they'd see each other alive at the plantation. When they did run into each other, the sisters celebrated with an all night chat in the field while everyone else slept. There would be many such midnight chats in the next few months. Despite their rivalry, my mother and her sister Thu enjoyed a good gossip session.

The plantation had acre after acre of rice paddies. But it had only four bamboo shacks for workers and one main house for the owner. The house contained five rooms. In those five rooms slept 10 families. Most people slept on bamboo mats, covering themselves with paper-thin sheets. Some lucky ones rocked themselves to sleep on hammocks, all the while enjoying the softness of real blankets. Aunt Thu, her family and Thu's brood of younger siblings shared one room. My mother, her husband Nam and Nam's sisters shared another room. The rest of the house lodged other relatives. One of those relatives happened to be Nam's good-looking cousin. Handsome Cousin couldn't believe his luck seeing my mother again at the plantation. Imagine, the object of his fantasy sleeping only one room away! With proximity came forbidden thoughts. Handsome Cousin exchanged sweet nothings with my mother during the day. At night, he wrote hard-core fantasies to satisfy his yearnings.

Uncle Hai hardly remembered the escape to the countryside. But he remembered well life at the plantation. Far from the sounds of rifle fire, he soon forgot the war and settled down to a life of routine. In the morning, he helped feed the chickens then collected water from the river. In the afternoon, he played with his nephew Kim. Family ties and physical closeness brought the two boys together. At the plantation, they thoroughly enjoyed each other's company. Innocence spared them the angst of war. Only once did the boys ask about Grandmother, Grandfather, Uncle Tan — family members who had stayed back in Hanoi.

Life at the plantation flew smoothly for Uncle Hai until the day he accidentally saw his quiet brother-in-law fumbling under the sheets. His two oldest sisters were chatting in the field that night. Unable to sleep, Uncle Hai decided to play a trick on his nephew Kim. He wanted to tickle Kim's feet. Uncle Hai crawled under the sheet, heading for Kim's legs. At that moment, he noticed his brother-in-law's hand on his sister Shirley. He didn't quite understand the scene; the man's hand inside the girl's pyjamas, but he knew it to be forbidden. Then Uncle Hai heard a muttering that troubled him even more. "Hmmm, so nice, she has no hair!" My six-year-old uncle couldn't quite grasp the perversity behind these words. Hair? There's hair down there? "Hair" as in "hairdo"? "Nice" as in "nice hairdo"? *What's the old man talking about?* Uncle Hai asked himself this question, which for a young boy, held no answers. Then he went to sleep perplexed. The next day, Uncle Hai developed a strange desire to play with Aunt Shirley's hair. "Let me braid your hair, make you nice hairdo!" he begged his sister. "What do you know about braiding hair? Leave me alone!" Aunt Shirley shouted.

My Aunt Shirley was named after Shirley Temple. Her curly hair framing chubby cheeks made her so white-looking, the American name stuck. Her singsong voice charmed all those around her. All in all, she acted as adorably as Shirley Temple herself. Unfortunately, Aunt Shirley's brain sang no sweet lyrics. No brightness emanated from there. In 1948, a 10-year-old Aunt Shirley left bullet-ridden Hanoi with her older sister Thu, Thu's husband and many other people. At the plantation, she had chores to do like everyone else. Being a bit older than Uncle Hai, she had to wash everyone's dirty clothes till her hands turned raw. She even washed her sister Thu's menstrual cloths. Thu's husband saw Shirley's thankless tasks every morning. He saw how his wife treated her own sister like a maid. He took pity on the young girl. He asked to see her raw hands. He took her hands in his, then rubbed a drop of cooking oil on her palms to ease the pain. After many hand rubbing sessions, he became bolder. One night, when his wife Thu left for the field with my mother, he approached Aunt Shirley. This was no hard task. The object of his fantasy slept only two mats away! The Pedophile told Shirley he would like to rub oil on her thighs plus "that place down there." Aunt Shirley acquiesced. She let him proceed for it felt good. She, too, knew this to be a forbidden game. She knew if her sister Thu found out she would be in trouble. Out of guilt, Aunt Shirley kept silent. Out of confusion, a perplexed Uncle Hai also kept quiet. Aunt Shirley was The Pedophile's first victim. There would be many more after that. He always preyed on the most vulnerable child at the most vulnerable time. He functioned best during periods of turmoil when matters of life and death took precedence over all else. During the 1948 battle against the French, The Pedophile showed his dirty hand at a rice plantation. He showed it again in a Saigon garage bunker during the battle of *Tet* '68. The Pedophile always made his victims feel guilty. Perverted minds functioned this way. They schemed to turn victims into silent collaborators.

Chapter 13

Mary the Teenager

When my cousin Daniel passed away in Montreal, two family members missed his funeral. Aunt Thu and her pedophile husband stayed home. In the days before anti-virals, we saw HIV as a modern plague. We feared catching Daniel's disease but we did gather for his funeral. For Aunt Thu and The Pedophile however, the spectre of the virus lingered long after the last breath.

The Pedophile feared diseases. He overdosed on multi-vitamins to ease his hypochondriac mind. He wanted to delay the day when his perversities would finally be exposed. He knew his victims would talk the minute he kicked the bucket. And he couldn't bear to have his good name stripped away on his deathbed. To outlive his young victims, he'd study my mother's medical texts for miracle cures. He harassed my mother for new treatments to imaginary maladies. The Pedophile loved his weekly vitamin B12 shots. He loved exposing his wrinkly ass to my doctor mother. The whole process titillated him — the cool rubbing alcohol on his skin, my mother's fingers pinching his droopy flesh, the addictive sensation of a needle inside his meat. The manipulation of his bum became a weekly show we couldn't escape.

We saw it performed on the living room sofa every Monday. To my mother's consternation, The Pedophile clamoured for more vitamin shots. My mother always gave in to his whining. Although The Pedophile played his dirty tricks in darkness, he also liked flashing his exhibitionist side to us.

❧

The Pedophile feared Daniel. He hated Daniel's long memory and intimate knowledge of our family's secrets. If he could, The Pedophile would erase those memories. But he knew he couldn't. He couldn't undo what he did to Aunt Shirley. He couldn't reprogram Uncle Hai's memory of that shameful act.

❧

Uncle Hai grew up full of complexes. The memory of his brother-in-law fingering his 10-year-old sister nagged at his conscience. He tried hard to repress that scene over the years. With time, he succeeded. He convinced himself those images came from a misty dream. He managed to carry on with the business of growing up in times of war. He treated The Pedophile as a normal human being. After all, this man had married his sister Thu. This man had fathered his nephew and best friend Kim. Outwardly, Uncle Hai showered The Pedophile with the utmost respect. But something inside him squirmed every time their hands met. Uncle Hai could never explain to himself this strange twist in his gut.

When my grandfather died, Uncle Hai's world came close to extinction. Witnessing his father's illness pained my uncle. He thought his French-educated doctor father capable of tricking Death. French medicines failing in their mission shocked a naive Uncle Hai. Like a faithful dog, the smell of despair followed the family everywhere. Two days after her husband's funeral, my grandmother ceased talking. In the first few months of her widowhood, she only said "Tuk, tuk" before returning to her betel chewing. Silence became the only sound heard at home.

Uncle Hai eventually emerged from his mourning. To forget his distressed state, a young Uncle Hai turned to girls for comfort. But his relationship with the opposite sex was far from healthy. He didn't fall in love, he didn't have crushes, he didn't even flirt. The relationships only consisted of sex and domination. Subconsciously, Uncle Hai re-enacted The Pedophile's fantasy, giving free rein to the old man's perversity. Without knowing it, Uncle Hai's first glimpse of sex — an adult hand inside a young girl's pyjamas — would influence his style forever. Innumerable ladies fell victim to my uncle's insatiable libido. But he was a victim himself.

To keep my mother company, Uncle Hai went with her to Dalat in 1960. Far from parental control, a teenaged Uncle Hai bloomed into a macho lover. Despite my mother's disapproving eyes, Uncle Hai daily entertained female classmates in his room. They all giggled when he took out his magic wand. My mother may have disapproved with her looks, but she kept her mouth shut. She knew well her new status in society. As an adulteress with a child out of wedlock, my mother stood on the same karma level as that of a cockroach. She certainly couldn't lecture her younger brother on the virtues of a Confucian family.

Of the giggling girls welcoming Uncle Hai's sperm, sixteen-year-old Mary giggled the loudest. No exceptional beauty marked her from the rest. But her sense of humour kept Uncle Hai entertained. Mary returned often enough to the house for my mother to remember her name. The other girls were only 'Pimple Face', 'Peach Fuzz', 'Big Boobs' or 'Knock Knees'. Unlike the other girls, Mary came from a devout religious family. While her father prayed to Jesus, her mother worshiped Buddha. Either way, Mary was doomed. Her pre-marital sexual acts guaranteed her both an afterlife in hell and a next-life as a worm. Despite the saintly name, there would be no virgin birth.

The early 60s were marked by frequent political protests in South Vietnam. But the country was still at peace. The streets of Saigon bustled with former French colonialists, new American Peace Corps types and a horde of international journalists in town to check the pulse of a soon-to-be media hot spot. The first wave of bars bloomed to entertain all these avid foreigners. Excitement filled the air. This was also a time of unreliable contraception and illegal abortions in Vietnam.

When Mary felt a kicking foot in her expanding womb, she immediately warned Uncle Hai. Just as immediately, Uncle Hai denied his role in the affair. "Mary is wild. She sleeps with other men. It's not my fault!" Uncle Hai protested to my mother as the news of Mary's pregnancy spread. Unfortunately, Mary's parents didn't share this opinion. Daily they pestered my mother for a quick solution to the problem. An unsafe illegal abortion was out of the question for them. A fast marriage to hush the gossipers was unacceptable in my mother's mind. My mother, who had wed a man she didn't love, couldn't force this marriage of convenience on her young brother. After much discussion, they decided to put the baby up for adoption.

To avoid the nastiness of idle tongues, Mary spent the rest of her pregnancy in a convent, which has been built exactly for such situations. Her teachers were notified of her "tuberculosis-like condition needing long term rest." An uneventful pregnancy gave Mary plenty of time to reflect on the down side of sex. With no visits from the outside world, she became despondent. She yearned for human contact, for freedom, for her former body. She wanted to be rid of this baby inside her, to resume her old student life.

Fifteen months after my birth, another unwanted child uttered his first cry in a Dalat clinic. Uncle Hai never bothered with paternal visits. Too afraid to admit responsibility, he convinced himself the baby resulted from some other man's sperm. Only my mother visited Mary at the clinic. She sympathized with Mary's predicament, feeling sorry for this younger version of herself. Here were two women fallen from grace, two bastard babies crying out for a paternal surname.

After an exhausting labour, Mary held the baby for fifteen minutes then fell asleep. When she woke the next day, the baby no longer shared her room. "It's at the orphanage," her mother told her. Mary sighed but did not ask for more details. She wished to forget motherhood. She wished to become a daughter again. A week after the delivery, Mary left the convent, returning home to her pet dog and textbooks. She never mentioned the baby again.

At the orphanage, Mary's baby grew in total indifference to the absence of love. He learned to steal other children's food to still the pangs in his stomach. He picked up bad words from the staff to swear at himself. At night, he rocked himself to sleep or banged his head on the bed's railings for attention. When a loose screw fell out of the crib, he didn't place it in his mouth like most toddlers would. He tried inserting it back into its hole instead. After many unsuccessful attempts, he hit the screw with his hand then licked the blood trickling from his bruised fingers.

My mother occasionally visited Mary's baby at the orphanage. Guilt and a sense of duty brought her there. She blamed herself for dragging Horny Uncle Hai to Dalat with her. Had he stayed in Saigon under Grandmother's watch, perhaps he wouldn't have been so wild. If she could have turned back the clock, my mother would have. She would have spared her younger brother the indignity of living the rest of his days a coward. She would have spared Mary the shame of an unwanted teenage pregnancy. Most importantly, she would have spared the baby a life of rejection and melancholy.

On her fifth visit to the orphanage, my mother decided on a whim to adopt Mary's baby. At two years old, he no longer needed diapers but still depended on a pacifier for quiet dreams. Scabs covered his bony legs. His big head over a disproportionally small body gave him an extraterrestrial aura. He clung to the nun's skirt, refusing my mother's outstretched arms. He screamed when my mother yanked his hand away. But his sad downcast eyes convinced my mother she had made the right decision. She couldn't leave him to rot in an orphanage. My cousin Tim became my brother the day Mother brought him home.

When my mother returned to Saigon with two fatherless children in her arms, Grandmother couldn't stop shaking her head. She muttered to herself all day. She stopped eating, losing 20 kilos in a few months. Grandmother didn't ask where the extraterrestrial came from. She suspected the worst from my mother. Were they two different kids from two different men? Or did they both come from that cursed cousin of hers, Buffalo Boy? It didn't matter. The damage to Grandmother's Confucian image had been done. Nothing my mother said could relieve Grandmother's sense of shame. Imagine Bad Luck and The Extraterrestrial in one house! Thank God for Frenchy Boy entertaining her with his tricks.

My mother's scandalous behaviour robbed Grandmother of her restful nights. Losing face to the world, she locked herself in the house. She refused visits from old friends, fearing their sweet and sour doubletalk. The most innocent inquiries from neighbours became daggers in

Grandmother's scheme of things. From shame, came paranoia. To escape both, my grandmother became a hermit. She refused to step out the front door.

❧

Uncle Hai never knew what some people knew about him. His state of denial prevented him from seeing clearly. When my mother brought Tim home, Uncle Hai couldn't put two and two together. Since he had forgotten Mary's pregnancy long ago, he never made the link between his own vigorous sperms and little tinkering Tim. Yet Tim sported the same physical attributes that made Uncle Hai so irresistible to young ladies: asymmetrical dimples and thick curly hair. In the days before DNA testing, this would have been enough proof for a paternity suit. But Uncle Hai remained impervious to the clues. "You're adopting a two-year-old kid?" Uncle Hai asked my mother. "Your own unwanted kid is not enough?" To this, my mother only sneered. She felt no need to explain the obvious to those blinded by self-absorption and fear.

Chapter 14

Aunt Frances and the Obsessive-Compulsive Lawyer

The day my cousin Daniel passed away, Tim became bloated with undigested ideas. Daniel never expanded on his 'Uncle Hai is your father' revelation. Somnolence prevented Daniel from talking during his last few days on earth. Decency wouldn't let Tim bug a dying man for explanations. And a funeral was no place to open a can of worms.

My mother kept Tim's origins a secret from most people. It gave her a sense of satisfaction knowing some loose tongues lost sleep trying to figure this one out. My mother never bothered with the adoption story. Nobody would believe her if she did. "Gutter women don't adopt babies! Especially when they already have an out-of-wedlock kid!" To argue against the dictum of the times would have been a waste of time. So my mother never bothered.

Only my mother's younger sister, Aunt Frances, knew the truth. Separated by a mere sixteen months, Aunt Frances shared many of my mother's deepest desires. As children sleeping in the same bed, they knew each other's softest spots. Rather than competing with each other, the two sisters complemented each other. Aunt Frances had a flawless China doll complexion with dimples to match. But a flat chest left some matchmakers unimpressed. My mother had a not-quite-perfect face, but her curvaceous body made up for the dimple-less smile. The two sisters drove young men to desperation with their 'don't bother me' air.

My grandmother excelled at force-feeding her daughters fixed marriages. So Aunt Frances, too, married a man she didn't love at fifteen. But fortunately for Aunt Frances, her husband carried himself decently in public. He didn't scratch himself all day. He didn't look like a monkey. He also came from a rich merchant family not satisfied with just owning land. Overseas education and foreign titles tickled their fancy. They went to sleep each day to the lullaby of Josephine Baker's *"J'ai deux amours, mon pays et Paris ..."* Like the American singer, these people also nurtured two loves: their country and Paris. Nightly, they dreamed of the City of Light despite the violence inflicted on their countrymen by French soldiers.

With its ebb and flow, the war occasionally lulled to sleep. A soldier's rest, a letting-down-of-the-guard during holidays — and my aunt managed to slip through checkpoints. With her husband, she succeeded in coming to Paris to live out her fantasy.

Aunt Frances' real name was Thuy Oanh. In Paris, she changed this Vietnamese tongue twister to "France" to ingratiate herself with her French landlady. At first, the landlady called my aunt "that Annamite, that Indochinese woman." Later, when she learned of my aunt's new name, she could no longer show such disrespect. After all, the landlady couldn't sneer at "that France woman" when she herself came from Algeria. When it became fashionable to speak English, even in chauvinistic Paris, my aunt added an "s" to her name. One day, out of the blue, she became Frances, just like the then famous American actress Frances Farmer.

Being away from Vietnam, Aunt Frances and her husband experienced few war-related sorrows. In Paris, the young couple made do in a one-room studio with a fireplace serving as stove. They got used to eating simple food but never got used to sharing a Turkish toilet with eight other tenants. In Vietnam, defecating meant going out to the field. On a nice day, this could be a pleasant experience. Sharing a stinking Turkish toilet with eight strangers was definitely not pleasant. Aunt Frances and her husband had no choice but to partake in this exercise of aiming their shit into a hole. Missing the hole meant splashing their shoes with the brown stuff. This introduction to unsanitary conditions turned Frances' husband into an obsessive-compulsive. He'd open doors with his elbows. He'd rub alcohol on all his clothes before wearing them. He'd get up in the middle of the night to sanitize the faucet handles. Their situation wasn't ideal, but Aunt Frances managed to pick up a half-baked form of French *savoir-faire* while her husband studied Napoleonic law. They befriended the French chambermaid Catherine and my Uncle Chinh. The two couples hit it off marvellously. Despite the cramped quarters, dirty toilets and a permanently grey sky, Aunt Frances grew to love her new city. Despite the tension created by the French Indochina War, no one shouted "Go Home!" to her husband. Despite their exotic looks, no one eyed them with suspicion. They blended into the mass of indifferent pedestrians walking the streets of Paris.

The extended stay in Paris left a pleasant taste on Aunt Frances' tongue. She became modern, open-minded, less rigid. Believing Aunt Frances to be less judgmental than the rest of the family, my mother opened up to her sister. The story of my father courting my mother despite the same blood in their veins, the retreat to Dalat to avoid curious eyes staring at her bulging stomach, Horny Uncle Hai's presence in Dalat to keep my mother company, his wild ways with girls, Mary's unwanted pregnancy, the birth of two bastard kids within fifteen months of each other — my mother unloaded all of this to her younger sister. My aunt might have lived in wild Paris, but she'd never heard so many soap operas in all her years there. "Please, keep all this secret," my mother pleaded. Too bewildered, Aunt Frances couldn't think of anything to say. She only nodded.

Of course, vows were made to be broken, secrets to be spread. Within a few months, Aunt Frances' husband became a witness to my mother's titillating story. But his obsessive-compulsive nature kept him from fantasizing about this unkempt woman. He imagined dousing her with rubbing alcohol first. And the thought of such acts suddenly tempered all his desires.

When her children became old enough to understand adults' twisted ways, Aunt Frances entertained them with my mother's immoral tale. And so the story spread, from one person to another, each one promising the other to keep it secret. This promise to keep things under lid prevented the tale from spreading like wildfire. After all, one couldn't promise to stay quiet then turn around blurting it out the next day. To give themselves credibility, these guardians of dark corners had to hold their tongues for a while before their gossiping nature took over. So my mother's tale spread but only at a snail's pace.

By the time the story reached my ears, I had celebrated my 26th birthday. I heard the story of Tim's origin from Aunt Frances' daughter. This girl, my cousin, shot heroin for emotional relief. Her father's use of elbows to open doors enraged my cousin. She detested his obsessive scrubbing of toilet seats five times a day. She reacted by spending days in the dirtiest of places — a shooting den where the most intimate bodily fluids passed indiscriminately from person to person. In her lucid moments, she would socialize with bug-infested beggars on the streets. She would bring them home to shower then steal from her mother's purse. So of course I didn't believe my cousin's words at first. The mixture of cocaine and heroin made her speech unintelligible. I also knew she lied compulsively so I crossed her off as completely unreliable. But when her mother, my Aunt Frances, confirmed the story, I could no longer dismiss it. Immediately, I shared the tale with my cousin Daniel who of course spread it to others. But there remained two persons who never knew the truth until it was too late for redemption: Horny Uncle Hai and my brother Tim.

My mother wished to hide the truth from Tim at all cost. She remembered Tim's head-banging obsession at the orphanage and wished to spare him all those desolate memories. Although she wanted him to grow up "normal," Tim never felt normal in our family. No matter how hard she tried, my mother could never overcome her natural instinct of preferring her own flesh and blood.

Tim grew up with a roof over his head, food in his mouth, clothes on his body. But despite repeated washings, the sad smell of hand-me-downs persisted. We spared him the indignity of wearing dresses, but my old flowery pants and lacy blouses in all shades of pink became a part of his regular wardrobe. Instead of indulging in the games Daniel and I played, my brother Tim preferred his own insular world. He played with Daniel's old broken toys. Amazingly, the broken toys didn't break my brother's spirit. They opened up a world of possibility for him instead. By screwing back loose car parts, Tim discovered a passion for fixing things. While my brother couldn't fix his own melancholia, he took pleasure in returning life to old lifeless objects.

Chapter 15

Aunt Shirley Temple

The day Daniel passed away in a Montreal hospital, Aunt Shirley huffed and puffed on the other side of the globe. Anger turned her breathing laborious. Anger had made an asthmatic of her years ago. When Aunt Shirley heard about The Pedophile's boycott of Daniel's funeral, she fumed even more. She thought her head would pop. Like Daniel in his last days on earth, Aunt Shirley pretty much hated everyone in the family. She especially hated The Pedophile. And she wanted everybody to know it.

Aunt Shirley was born a pretty young girl with curly hair. In the days before war and displacement, she sang like the real Shirley Temple. After the 1948 exodus to safer ground, Aunt Shirley returned to Hanoi almost a dwarf. No one recognized her. No one could explain this stunted growth. "Shirley caught cholera at the rice plantation," Aunt Thu told Grandmother. "Maybe that's why she stopped growing." Grandmother didn't seem convinced. Uncle Hai caught cholera as a kid, too. He grew normally. Why not Shirley?

Besides Uncle Hai, no one else knew of The Pedophile's dirty tricks at the plantation. These filthy acts didn't occur once or twice. They occurred on a regular basis. The Pedophile

117

never hurt Aunt Shirley. He never tried raping her. He only touched her most secret spots. A naturally hairless Mound of Venus — this was his weakness. Aunt Shirley never complained. Those touching sessions gave her rest from her chores. She also enjoyed the massages. Yet, despite her young age, Aunt Shirley knew the whole thing smelled of perversity. They shouldn't be doing this. Her brother-in-law shouldn't be fingering her in his wife's absence. Unfortunately, Aunt Shirley was too young to call guilt by its name. She never experienced this unpleasantness before. Unbeknownst to her, this weight on her conscience, this guilt, not able to find an external outlet, would turn inward to affect her physiology and stunt her growth.

When Aunt Shirley became old enough to recognize guilt, she decided to use it to wipe her ass. Why should she feel guilty for The Pedophile's crime? Why should she blame herself for his wife's ostrich behaviour? With time, Aunt Shirley's childhood guilt transformed itself into hate. Her Shirley Temple voice became the voice of bitterness. From a cute girl, she grew up to look like a sitting Sitting Bull. In her twenties, Aunt Shirley was the only unmarried girl in the family.

❧

In 1958, Aunt Shirley worked for my mother at her French restaurant *Aux Délices*. Since my mother didn't trust strangers with the handling of her money, she put Aunt Shirley at the cash register. When things got busy, Aunt Shirley also helped out at the bar. She poured drinks to lonely sailors on weekend leave. She listened to tales of faraway lands and developed itchy feet. Whenever a drunken soldier complimented her on her curls, she felt the itchiness in her crotch rising. Any woman in her right mind would take a drunken sailor's words with a grain of salt. Aunt Shirley took them as a lifeline. "Hey Baby! Want to suck my dick?" In her heart, Aunt Shirley heard "Do you want to be rescued from this family?" The answer would be a resounding yes.

One sailor who returned often to court Aunt Shirley came by way of Somalia. As a not-so-devout black Muslim, Mahamoud stood out from the crowd. Mahamoud's luscious African lips aroused in Aunt Shirley all kinds of hidden desires. For once, she could forget The Pedophile's hand. For the first time in her life, she thought of sex as pleasure, not as guilt.

While Aunt Shirley lived out her fantasy, Grandmother lived through her miseries. Like most Orientals of her generation, Grandmother filled her head with racist nonsense. She couldn't welcome a black son-in-law into the family. The more Grandmother tried changing her daughter's mind, the more Aunt Shirley stood her ground. When "I'll kill myself if you marry that man!" didn't work, Grandmother tried other tactics. "You're no longer my daughter if you marry that man!" Grandmother threatened. To this, Aunt Shirley only said, "Fine!" "Get out of our lives then!" Grandmother screamed, then immediately regretted her words. Their fragile mother-daughter relationship ended with a slammed door.

To escape curious eyes and loose tongues, Aunt Shirley also moved to Dalat with her Muslim Hunk. There, she almost died giving birth to her daughter. The bleeding would not stop. The lost blood turned Aunt Shirley into a white sheet, yet no one came to comfort her. Muslim Hunk worked out of town that day. Her family had already closed the door to tenderness years ago. If Aunt Shirley had died on the delivery table that rainy afternoon, no family member would have been witness to her sorrows. Fortunately, Aunt Shirley survived.

In Dalat, my Aunt Shirley raised two chocolate-coloured children with Muslim names. For a few months, Aunt Shirley also stopped eating pork. She thought she could sever family ties this way. But family ties, like cultural roots, dug deep. They spread beyond name and food choices. My aunt couldn't undo this heritage, even with Muslim Hunk's luscious lips on her pubis.

Aunt Shirley's marriage ended in an amiable separation after four years. As it turned out, Muslim Hunk was still married to three other women in Somalia. He also fathered a brood of children, all of them claiming rights to his salary. Although she loved his African lips, my aunt could no longer tolerate his deceitful talk. Unfortunately, Muslim Hunk was no lifeline for Aunt Shirley.

To avoid her mother's I-told-you-so grin, Aunt Shirley hopped on a ship with her no-longer beloved. They headed for his home country of Somalia. In Africa, Muslim Hunk granted my aunt custody of their children on the condition that she would never serve them pork. To support her kids, Aunt Shirley worked in restaurants, serving Vietnamese food to fellow colonized Africans. After years of toiling under the hot Somali sun, of living in a bare hut and sleeping on a dirt floor, Aunt Shirley got fed up. She remembered she was once the daughter of a doctor. Nostalgia for the Hanoi mansion of her childhood filled her nights. If she couldn't return to Vietnam, a single mother with chocolate-coloured children, she could certainly go to France like her sister Frances. As dreams of Paris fuelled her heart, Aunt Shirley began to sing again. But deception soon soured her singsong voice. With no formal education, my aunt could only find menial jobs in Paris. She could only continue to toil. While Aunt Frances enjoyed an indolent life as wife of a successful lawyer, Aunt Shirley made her living as an underpaid housekeeper. Day in, day out, she cleaned Parisians' chamber pots.

Despite her bad luck in life, Aunt Shirley hung on. She never developed serious psychological dysfunction. She only developed diabetes. She ate to still the anger in her soul, but the food only made her fat. It never put a smile on her face. And as Aunt Shirley grew fatter, she looked shorter. In Paris, Aunt Shirley befriended an unemployed melancholic Frenchman. One day, the Frenchman became suicidal in her absence. To spare the neighbours the consequences of his act, the Frenchman set himself on fire in the bathtub. When firemen came into the bathroom, they only found a charred body. Everything else remained intact. The neighbours expressed shock but also relief that the fire hadn't spread. When the news reached Aunt Shirley, she gave a loud curse. Then she went back to scrubbing her client's toilet. By this time, Aunt Shirley had given up on hope of a better life.

Aunt Shirley didn't hate life. She just hated most of the people in her life. Besides her own children, she had little tolerance for others. The mention of Grandmother's name made her blood boil. She hated The Pedophile and Aunt Thu with a passion. My mother's medical career also rubbed my aunt the wrong way. *If an adulterous woman can turn her life around, why can't I do the same?* Aunt Shirley would ask herself this every night. Every morning, the answer would evade her.

With her soul marinated in resentment, Aunt Shirley found it hard to socialize. She spoke little, rarely laughed, answered the phone only between six and seven pm. While she avoided her siblings, Aunt Shirley did feel sympathy for my cousin Daniel and my brother Tim. She could identify with the hole in their hearts. Here were three destinies hijacked by maternal indifference.

Tim met Aunt Shirley for the first time in Paris. As a student hiking through Europe in the 1980s, my brother welcomed the occasional free bed. Although she hardly talked, Tim found Aunt Shirley likable. For reasons unknown to him, my brother felt an affinity for this fat, midget aunt.

Aunt Shirley knew of Tim's origins. The regretted sperm, the unwanted pregnancy, the orphanage story — she had witnessed it all because she, too, had lived in Dalat in 1960. Like my mother, Aunt Shirley disappeared from Saigon society after overstepping the narrow boundaries of that time and place. As sinners giving a bad name to their family, the sisters knew they had to hide. My mother sinned for sharing a bed with her married cousin. Aunt Shirley sinned for loving a black man against her family's wishes. The Vietnamese mentality of the times allowed them no redemption. In Dalat, the two sisters limited their contact. Too busy with their own misfortunes to spare a thought for the other, they communicated through greeting cards. Aunt Shirley occasionally visited my mother when Muslim Hunk went out of town. My mother never returned those visits. Brainwashed by Grandmother's poison, my mother could never bring herself to enter a black person's house.

During those Parisian afternoons shared with Tim, Aunt Shirley might have been tempted to download the truth. But she held back. We all held back. We all kept the truth from Tim. We knew we couldn't deliver this 26-year-old message properly. Only Horny Uncle Hai could. But Postman Hai never rang.

Tim finally confronted my mother a week after Daniel's death. Pushed into a corner, my mother could no longer hide. She gave Tim her version of the truth. Like all children given up for adoption, he wanted to know one thing: Why? "Because your mother was only sixteen" didn't suffice. This easy answer hardly satisfied his yearnings. My mother soon realized that no explanation could fill the fissures in Tim's heart. Without knowing why, Tim felt an absence all his life. He couldn't name what he lacked, but the craving had always been there. Now with the secret revealed, my brother felt even lonelier. He wished he could cry for a childhood full of emptiness. But no tears flowed.

Chapter 16

My Grandmother Anh

My grandmother died in Montreal at the age of 103. When she passed away in 2005, she had outlived her husband, her son Tan, her grandson Daniel, her second cousin Buffalo Boy and her daughter's eternal admirer, Handsome Cousin. We knew she carried good genes but we didn't know they could be that resistant. Seeing my grandmother in her coffin reminded me of my great-grandmother's story. How could I forget the tale of Great-Grandmother outliving her fake sandalwood coffin?

Like my great-grandmother, Grandmother thought she'd die at ninety. Then at ninety-five. Then at ninety-nine. She saw signs of her demise everywhere. One day, when her indoor violets unexpectedly bloomed in late winter, she shivered in resignation. "I will die this year!" Grandmother told her children. When that didn't happen, she said: "Don't worry, the end isn't far!" Her longevity became a source of both pride and shame. Grandmother felt proud of her good genes, her healthy body, her quick wits. Yet shame for living so long also weighed on her spirit. She didn't want to be a nuisance to her children. Passing the year 2000 seemed a big ordeal. Grandmother dreaded the Year 2000 Bug. When the world didn't collapse on January 1, 2000, Grandmother gave up her predictions.

In 2001, Grandmother turned her attention to politics instead. She became a fan of both George W. Bush and Canadian Prime Minister Jean Chretien. She saw no contradiction in this conflicting allegiance. Grandmother saw the Twin Towers' destruction as a sign from God. "Repent! The end of the world is near," she would repeat incessantly at family gatherings. Of course, we didn't take her words seriously. But we couldn't dismiss her either. She had a way of saying ridiculous things that turned out true later. In 1980, we all laughed when Grandmother said: "The Communists are here but they will disappear. Buddha said so! You wait and see!" When the Berlin wall collapsed a few years later, we had to agree with Grandmother's "I told you so!"

My grandmother was not an exceptionally intelligent woman, but years of reading French newspapers had shaped her opinions on almost every subject. Her old age also gave her a sense of mystical wisdom. Even if I laughed at Grandmother's predictions on the end of the world, I took her warning seriously. I found it impossible to do otherwise. The media bombarded us with tragic news footage in the days after Sept 11. And the more I saw, the more I wanted to see. Images of death and destruction so near to home brought back painful memories of the Vietnam War years. For a few weeks after September 11, the world seemed on the verge of ending for me.

Unbeknownst to me at the time, my niece's future husband would be one of the last ones to flee the second crumbling building that fateful September morning. He would later marry, have children and attend many more marriages. So Grandmother erred after all. The world did not end after September 11.

My grandmother lived a hundred years of solitude. She witnessed firsthand the scourge of the 20th century. She personally experienced the scars of colonialist rule, wars, displacement, disease and the disintegration of an orderly world. Her personal life was afflicted by death and scandals. But Grandmother kept a straight face through it all. She never doubted her spiritual belief in Buddha. Until she became bedridden the last months of her life, Grandmother never forgot her daily offering of tea to Buddha.

Chanting Buddhist monks in saffron robes came for Grandmother's funeral. Montreal's Vietnamese expat community gathered to give their respect. We all mourned the passing away of our family's matriarch. My grandmother was no saint, we all knew that. With her old-fashioned, domineering, racist and interventionist attitude, she brought grief to many of us. In return, she suffered enormously from our cavalier behaviour. A vicious circle, unbreakable even in death, glued us together.

With Daniel and Grandmother gone, there would be no more stories to tell. Silence would keep the next generation ignorant of their history. In North America, my children lead generally normal lives. They follow the dramas of reality TV stars on television. They spend hours on Facebook, photoshopping their life stories. In their search for identity, they Google themselves. But identities aren't found on the Internet. They are found in the words passed from one generation to the next. These family narratives, so perverse yet fascinating, scream out to be heard ... This history of a country the world once noticed but now forgets deserves to be retold.

This tale is for them, the next generation.

Chapter 17

The Family Ten Years Later

In her old age, my mother becomes afflicted with health problems. Her medical knowledge becomes a handicap. Instead of helping her see clearly, the medical training turns her into a hypochondriac. She thinks she recognizes all the symptoms of all the diseases in her body. But her body is only crying out for love. When her French-Canadian boyfriend left her for a younger woman in 1997, my mother experienced rejection for the first time. In her seventies, she is unprepared to face solitude. Stooping, with white hair, my mother no longer attracts men. The attention she had so freely as a young woman now escapes her grip. To compensate, she locks herself into a delusion of sickness. And being sick gives her the attention she needs.

In his old age, Horny Uncle Hai feels the responsibility of fatherhood for the first time. Although he has never opened up to Tim, he has changed his ways after the birth of Tim's daughter. He sends the girl a birthday gift every year. This is more than he ever did for Tim. The birthday gifts are a form of recognition. The gifts don't say: "I love you." They only say, "I have a granddaughter." It is better than nothing. After his many love conquests, Uncle Hai ends up living his old age with a size 42 D cup Canadian woman. She cooks for him and puts up with his tantrums. At seventy, The King of Mama's Boys still longs for his mother's breasts.

❧

In her old age, Aunt Thu congratulates herself for being the only one in the family still living a Confucian life. Her marriage to The Pedophile is the only one still intact in the family. There are times when she'd rather chop him to pieces. He started by molesting young family members. He ended up having affairs with his fifteen-year-old students. Aunt Thu isn't blind. Yet she tolerates his sticky fingers, his wandering penis. She wants to maintain an impeccable image of a dutiful wife at all cost. They celebrate their sixtieth wedding anniversary in a Montreal Chinese restaurant with pomp and circumstance. Fifty guests are invited, none of them knows of The Pedophile's perverted past. While the guests celebrate her sixty years of marriage, Aunt Thu secretly curses her sixty years of hypocrisy.

❧

In his old age, The Pedophile spends much time watching soft porn on pay television. He replaces his passion for the camera with a new hobby: landscaping. He can turn a plain patch of grass into an Oriental miniature garden. Neighbours noticed this interesting transformation and called a local journalist. When the cameras come for him, The Pedophile develops cold feet. "Thu, talk to them for me! I don't know what to say!" "Yes, my Other Half!" Although he loves the camera, he hates being in front of it. The Pedophile fears exposure. Like all pedophiles, he prefers working in hidden places. He will always be a worm.

❧

In his old age, Uncle Chinh becomes easily irritated. After years of seeing his Vietnamese second wife rejected by the family, he gives up. He can't understand their dismissive attitude towards her unpolished manners. Catherine, the French first wife, only held a chambermaid's certificate of excellence. Yet the family loved her. Why can't they love the second wife? Is the family racist towards their own kind? Or are they bound by loyalty to the memory of another era? Uncle Chinh is tired trying to figure this one out. So he spends his old age avoiding family contact. He stills refuses putting a name to his son's disease. More than thirty years after Daniel's death, Uncle Chinh still calls it hemorrhoids. Three decades later, Uncle Chinh still blames Daniel for his love of penises. He can neither forgive nor forget.

❧

In her old age, Aunt Frances tastes despair for the first time. One beautiful summer day, her daughter died a junkie on the streets of Paris. The drug-addicted daughter was a source of shame for 20 years. With a body ravaged by Hepatitis B and arms deformed by the scars of multiple suicide attempts, my cousin was an ugly sight to behold. Aunt Frances often wished her daughter success during those wrist-slashing frenzies. But wishful thinking is one thing, reality another. When death actually showed its black face, my aunt's world collapsed. Grief has since erased her dimples and sunny disposition. Aunt Frances, who moved to France at an early age, who experienced neither war nor poverty in her lifetime, became the face of pain after that summer. The family's bad luck had caught up with her.

❧

In her old age, Aunt Shirley gives free rein to her hoarder instinct. She collects bits of old newspapers. She refuses to throw out empty cans. Years of poverty in Africa taught her the usefulness of every bit of trash. She crams the junk in boxes then crams the boxes under her bed. Every inch of free space in her tiny Paris apartment is taken up by these packages of useless memories. The boxes serve as a fortress for Aunt Shirley, a fortress to protect her from the wandering hands of a pedophile so long ago.

❧

And me? I spent half a century searching for the ideal father figure, for a Handsome Cousin who would write me 20-page love letters then bring me to Australia. That love was found then lost in a tragic accident one sweltering summer day. To ease the sting, I followed in my family's footsteps. I took up medicine after dabbling in psychology. The balm I applied to my patients' burned bodies became an ointment for my own spirit. I now write 20-line e-mails and travel in my virtual world, trying to recreate a universe long dispersed by the winds of change. Like millions other ants, I struggle in my climb up the hill. But I survive the spirit of the time by going with the flow.

Acknowledgements

*I want to thank all the wonderful people
who made this book possible.*

My sincere thanks to:

*Michael Mirolla for his patience and skilful
editing. Ian Shaw for his encouragement
and invaluable suggestions.*

*Timothy Niedermann for his meticulous
copyediting. Lin Lin Mao and David Moratto
for the compelling cover art.*

My family for allowing me to tell this tale.

About The Author

Caroline Vu was born in Vietnam during the height of the Vietnam War. She left her native country at the age of 11, moving first to the US, then to Canada. In Montreal, the author graduated from McGill University with a degree in political philosophy. She went on to study psychology at Concordia University and medicine at the University of Montreal. After extended stays in Latin America and Europe, the author is back in Montreal where she lives with her two daughters. She currently works as a family physician in a community health clinic. Caroline was a freelance writer for *The Medical Post*, *The Tico Times*, and *The Toronto Star*. Her debut novel *Palawan Story* — published by Deux Voiliers Publishing in 2014 — was a finalist for the Concordia University First Book Prize.

Printed by Imprimerie Gauvin
Gatineau, Québec